That Smile of Yours

By Frank Yang

That Smile of Yours

1

I was lightly jogging home from school under the shining sun. Even though it was already spring, the occasional gentle breeze sent chills down my spine and made me tighten my jacket. I decided to take a nice walk in the city and enjoy myself because I was only in fifth grade.

As I waited for a traffic light, I glanced up at the skyscrapers on both sides of the street, wondering how in the world did the builders construct such feats. Suddenly, my mother's voice echoed in my head, "Kai, you're not a little kid anymore. You have to start thinking about your future. Think about what you want to be when you grow up and what'll your job be."

"I wonder what my life would be like if I became an architect." I asked myself. "I bet it'll be really fun!" Slowly at first, I heard a low rumbling coming from behind me. I thought it was a building construction because they were not uncommon in urban areas. But after a little bit, I realized that the noise was coming from the sky above. I gasped as soon as I saw the phenomenon before me. There were little red dots flying across the sky. But as they got closer and closer, I realized that they were five boulders, their sizes ranging from busses to small buildings, about to make contact with the ground. "Meteors..." I murmured, my body shaking uncontrollably in fear. I had no experience on how to deal with these real-life emergencies. As a result, all I could do was stare at the rocks in horror, my chances of survival dwindling by the second.

Soon, many of the people around me noticed the shooting stars as well. They began to panic and scramble in all different directions, looking for protection; I was not an exception. My survival instincts kicked in and I took off running, my brain spinning at high speed. I knew that there were two options. The first one was to sprint on the road and pray I can make it out of the collision zone in time. The second option was to duck under some cover, preferably a basement and do my best on reducing the impact damage with cushions. As soon as these two ideas popped into my head, I eliminated option one due to the amount of heavy traffic blocking the road and sidewalk. I turned around and hopped across a fence into someone's backyard and placed my back against the wall of the building and hoped for the best.

Immediately after making sure I was safe, I thought about my family; I had forgotten about them in the heat of the moment. My mother, father, and my little sister, Mia, I feared for their safety. "I hope they also saw the meteors and are evacuating properly." I sighed heavily, glancing up at the street. Sirens were blaring, cars were colliding into others and ramming into buildings. Panicking civilians were cramping into evacuation shelters and yelling. "They're not gonna get anywhere if they don't have any order among themselves..." My words were suddenly interrupted by a huge explosion, followed by the ground's loud tremoring.

My ears were ringing. My eardrums felt as if they were about to explode. "Please God...please." I clenched onto the nearby telegraph pole and refused to give in. But it was then, amidst all the clamoring and shouting surrounding me, I heard a faint cry coming from behind me. When I spun around, I caught sight of the silhouette standing right next to a crumbling building which was about to collapse.

She was a girl around my age, her frozen figure completely contradicted all the anxiety and action happening around her. There was something about her that caught my attention.

Perhaps it was her unreal calmness, or perhaps it was something else, I couldn't help myself on what I did next. "Ah! You've gotta be kidding me!" As if I've forgotten everything around me, I dashed to the girl as fast as I could without tripping over and put my hand onto her shoulder. "What are you doing? Quit standing around! Hurry up! Let's get outta here!"

"Why?" The girl whispered with a pair of watery eyes.

Confused, I asked, "Huh?"

"Why did they...?" As if getting choked up by her own words, she stopped midway through her sentence.

"They? Who are they?" Although we were running out of time, whomever she was talking to must be really important to her. Important enough that she would die for, but before her mouth had a chance to open, the answer was already lying right in front of me. Lying on the ground, were the corpses of two adults, their visages and their hair has been dyed bright red by their own blood. Their lifeless bodies not moving an inch, the light of life had already vanished from their eyes. "Oh" Too shocked to say anything, I managed to squeeze this word out of my mouth.

She sighs, "What's the point in living anymore?"

I looked up at the building directly over us, which was about to crush us to smithereens any second now, and screamed, "I'm sorry, but you're not dying here!"

"I don't care anymore."

I groaned in frustration. "I'm Kai. What's your name?" I said trying to make conversation to ease her pain. I took a few deep breaths and declared in a firmer voice, "Nevermind about it right now. I'm really sorry about your parents, but just because they died in an accident doesn't mean you have to end up the same way." I gulped nervously and continued, "I'm sure you can find happiness somewhere else in life! Y-you can even talk to me! I'd be happy to become friends with you once this is over! That's a promise! Even though there will be hard times, you have to keep smiling as you greet the future! So please! Come with me! Your parents wouldn't want you to die here as well!"

As soon as I mentioned her parents, her tense expression weakened. Tears began to well up in her eyes."To keep smiling...no matter what." She muttered. "W-why are you helping me? Your own life is on the line as well."

"Strange question...Why am I risking my life?" I asked myself, but before I even had a chance to think about it, the answer spilled uncontrollably out of my mouth.. "Because I can't live knowing that I could've saved someone, but didn't. I just can't live with that conscience! So please! You were alive for all these years! You were happy for all these years! Think about those times! How wonderful would it be if you can experience more fun times like that in the future!"

Her body jerked slightly, and as if finally grasping the value of life, she finally whispered, "I-I don't want to die..."

"Do you trust me?" I asked.

"I-I don't know why, but yes, I do." She muttered quietly.

"Then just take my hand, and we'll make it out of here alive."

With a slight nod, she raised her hand and clutched mine with all her might, not letting go. Her strength demonstrated the complete opposite of her wavering voice from before.

Miraculously enough, neither of us got seriously injured from the explosion, we were only a little shaken up. Once the ground stopped shaking, I took a deep breath, and grinned "See? We're fine."

However, we let down our guard too soon. The explosion flung debris and dust our way. The shockwave entirely obscured the sunlight. "Hold your breath!" I hollered, "Let's try to get into a shelter first." The sand and dirt would sometimes get into our eyes and mouths, but we somehow managed.

As we ran across the neighborhood to find the nearest safe building, I noticed the significant damage the disaster had caused. On either side of the road, many buildings were in flames, some already collapsed, especially many skyscrapers and taller buildings. Not only that, the explosion and impact left the street in shambles, making it even harder for us to escape. Even though we would stumble once in a while, we would always lend out a helping hand when the other fell.

I heard many screamings and painful yellings that day. People kneeling next to the corpse of the person they loved, crying their heart out. For other survivors, they went inside the remains of their houses to salvage any undamaged items. Prayers and mournings resounded throughout the entire neighborhood. I gritted my teeth as we ran past them, intentionally avoiding looking at the calamity surrounding me.

We finally made it to a shelter after five minutes of running. We were both out of breath by the time we got there. When we finally steadied our footsteps, I turned around and asked, "I don't think you told me, but what's your name?"

"Oh, sorry. I'm Ariya." The girl smiled as she answered . "My name's Ariya. Nice to meet you, Kai."

Although It was merely a simple gesture of happiness, her smile was genuine, free of worries and packed with feelings and appreciation. I etched it deep into my mind so I would never forget how beautiful it was.

"Ariya." I muttered the name aloud and smiled, fulfilled. As if that one word was enough to compensate for everything I did to her.

Before I could say anything else, however, I heard a loud rumbling next to us and the giant stone column began to sway and collapsed.

I didn't know the reason for what I did next, but perhaps it was the same reason for me helping her in the first place; I dashed directly at her and pushed her out of harm's way. But I was not so lucky, as I felt an excruciating pain in my legs, the stone structure crashed directly onto me.

The last thing I remember before losing consciousness was a pool of red engulfing me and Ariya kneeling next to me, gently whispering my name in her soft voice, over and over. "Kai...Kai..."

4 years later (Present 2020)

"Ariya!" I screamed aloud as I sat up from my bed, my entire body covered in sweat. I quickly shook my head and mumbled, "Oh Gosh! That was something that happened four years ago! Why am I having nightmares about it now?"

The truth was, I had plenty of reasons to remember such a dramatic moment in my life. After all, that meteor shower was how more than one thousand people lost their lives, including my father. I wasn't able to sleep for two entire weeks after finding out the tragic news. But that's not the worst. His death left a bigger scar in my little sister, Mia. He was only her foster parent, but it was understandable, considering that she had lost her "guardians" once before at a young age and had to go through the whole trauma again. After his death, Mia and my mother were put into a "sanctuary", built for the sole purpose of housing the refugees of the "Meteor Shower of 2016" because our old house had been completely smothered by the meteors..

However, I got separated from Mia because I was one of the only two people who were directly exposed to the radiation of the meteors and live. The other survivor being Ariya. I was taken away to a facility, and they performed many so-called "scientific," but disgraceful experiments on me. After spending about a year in the lab, I was excused to go to the outside world and see Mia and my mom again. The government granted us new homes following my return. Even though it was smaller than our previous home, it was plenty for three people. Since my mother would usually go on business trips to support the family all by herself, both Mia and I would pitch in and help out around the house because we knew we were on our own. My sister handled the cooking, and I took care of mostly everything else.

The house had two floors. The kitchen, living room, dining room, a bathroom, and a bedroom were on the first floor. The second floor had two bedrooms and a study, along with two bathrooms. Instead of constructing the building out of concrete before the incident, it was decided to build it out of wood as they were afraid of another incident.

I glanced at the clock in my room, the time read 6:30. "Ugh." I groaned quietly, "The first day of school is always the worst." I pushed open the window to let some fresh air into the room, but the leaves of the branches outside blocked most of the sunlight.

After changing into my school uniform, combing my hair, which had a crew cut because I rarely take care of it, I headed downstairs to the kitchen for breakfast. "Morning, Mia." I mumbled as my sister, jumped up from her chair energetically and greeted me. Her short brown hair flowed to just above her shoulders. Her brown eyes dazzled as she stared into mine.

"So what did you make for breakfast today?" I asked.

"Your favorite! Because it's your first day of school, right?" Mia said with a huge smile on her face. "It's grilled cheese!"

"Thanks." I said as I sat down in a chair next to the kitchen table and took a bite into the sandwich. "This is really good!" I exclaimed and patted Mia on the head.

She resisted at first, or at least pretended to resist and claimed that she was no longer a little kid and didn't want to be petted anymore. She loosened her grip on my arm and a satisfying smile appeared on her face when the palm of my hand touched her dark brown hair.

"Ahhh! Stop that!" Mia yelled and quickly drew her head back.

I decided to change the topic because I didn't want to get into an argument first thing in the morning. "You don't start school until next week because you're still in middle school, right?"

"Yup! Hehe, lucky me! I have one more week of free time! But you, on the other hand, have to suck it up and go to school!" She replied with a triumphant laugh on her face.

"Ugh." I grumbled, annoyed. "What grade are you gonna be in? Seventh?"

"Yea! I'm kinda nervous though." Mia muttered.

I lightly slapped her on the forehead. "Hey, at least you have friends. There's nothing I can do in school besides moping around."

"Kai, you're always so pessimistic. It's a brand new school. There's going to be a lot of new people! I'm sure you'll get along with someone."

"Oh yeah, what's that boy's name? Rick? Was it? Did you two work out?" I asked, remembering that a few days ago Mia told me that she was starting to show interest in a kid that just moved onto our street. They've already planned to be in the same class in the same school and had been hanging out.

"Kinda…" She replied hesitantly, her face slightly blushing.

"Well, lucky you. You're getting into a relationship even before your older brother." I chuckled.

"Maybe that's what you're missing this entire time. Once you find someone you care about, you'll start to enjoy the world around you." .

The morning sun finally made its way into the interior of the building and illuminated the room. "I hope so." I whispered quietly as I stuffed the remaining part of the sandwich into my mouth, "Mia, how long have we known each other for?"

"Huh? Oh… I dunno. Seven years? But if you don't count the year you were taken away…" Her voice trailed off to an end as she instantly put her hand over her mouth, not letting another word escape. "Oh. I'm sorry, I know we agreed to never mention that year in a conversation and to keep it a secret. My bad."

"That's okay. It's my fault for bringing up the topic anyways." I mumbled with a mouthful of food. "Well, looks like I'm done here. I guess I'll just… head to school now."

I got up from my chair, grabbed my backpack and started to head out the door. Before leaving, I look back at my sister and yelled, "Don't trash the house while I'm gone!"

"Okay!" Already back to her original mood, Mia yelled back. "Bye!"

The walk to school was only about five minutes because I practically lived right next to the campus. As I strolled along the sidewalk, I noticed a few buildings were still under reconstruction because of the damage caused by the Meteors. My high school was known for having one of the most beautiful campuses in the city. The two academic buildings, Science building, Music building, and Arts building surrounded a "central park" area the students could hang out in.

I had checked the school website for the classes I had been assigned to. And according to my schedule, I was supposed to meet up with my advisor, Mr. Eric, for the first period this morning. I walked into the white main academic building and headed into my classroom, numbered 1-4. Each number stood for a different grade; 1 was freshmen, 2 was sophomore, and so on.

As I walked down the hallway on the first floor of the building, I started seeing some familiar faces from my two years of middle school. However, to my surprise, there were also a lot of new kids as well. I turned right after reaching the end of the hallway and found the locker with my name printed on it, which happened to be right next to my classroom. I hung my jacket inside my locker before entering the classroom. By the time I entered, it was already mostly full of students. "Good morning." I muttered. A few classmates waved at me even though I had no idea who they were.

"Ah! And who might you be?" Said a large man with a very tanned skin color sitting behind the teacher's desk. His towering body even made my slightly above-average height look short.

"I'm Kai." I answered politely, shocked. "And… you're Mr. Eric?"

"Yeah! Why are you so surprised though?" He asked.

"I think you'd do better as a sports teacher than an advisor. Because of your muscular build and everything."

He started chuckling, "Believe me, this isn't the first time I've heard that suggestion. Anyways, go find yourself a seat and get ready. Class starts in five minutes."

"He's pretty funny. I think I'm pretty lucky I was put into his class." I thought to myself. *"Maybe this school year wouldn't be so boring after all."*

"Morning, Ben." I gestured to one of the students sitting at the back of the room. He was one of the few kids I got along well with back in middle school. He was much taller than I was and had bright red hair combed to one side. He had a strong jawline and glowing skin. His large blue eyes were warm and compassionate. Ben also had a thin mouth that revealed blinding white teeth.

"How was your summer?" Ben waved back as he closed the book he was reading.

"Stayed indoors the whole time and played video games." I sighed.

"Sounds like you." He smiled.

I was curious about his summer, but his phone rang before I could broach the subject. "I'll let you take care of it." I said as I walked up to the front of the room to the list of students hanging on the whiteboard. I wanted to check if there were other students other than Ben that I knew. As soon as I saw the name of the person on the top of the list, I stopped cold and took a deep breath.

"You've gotta be kidding me…" I muttered nervously, still couldn't believe what I just saw. "This isn't her, right? This surely has to be a mere coincidence."

"Kai? What's wrong? You got all excited all of a sudden. " Mr. Eric asked from his desk at the back of the classroom.

"N-nothing!" I shook my head and faked a smile on my face as I plopped myself down in a seat on the third row of the classroom with the window to my left.

Mr. Eric lightly shrugged, "If you say so."

There were four columns and five rows of desks, which meant that this was a medium-sized class of twenty students. I desperately scanned the room for the person I was looking for, but no luck, she wasn't there. As the bell rang signaling the beginning of class, I signed and mumbled, "Maybe it's just a coincidence in names."

"Let's see…" Mr. Eric said as he walked up to the front of the room. "Class is starting, but we're still missing a person."

"It still might be her." I thought to myself. *"There's still a chance."*

"Whatever. Whoever's late can just take the open seat to the right of Kai." Eric projected a powerpoint onto the board, but then got distracted by footsteps coming from the door in the back. "Oh, nevermind. She's here."

There, standing in the doorway, was a girl with blond hair, her slim figure dressed in a white skirt school uniform. Many of the boys in the class started murmuring about her dazzling beauty.

"Sorry I'm late, I got caught in traffic this morning." She said,

As soon as she opened her mouth, I recognized the familiar voice. It was a voice that brought back painful memories about the tragedy of my parent. But even so, I was really glad to hear it again.

As if throwing away all the boring things life has to offer, as if finding the light that will illuminate my path, uncontrollably, her name flowed out of my mouth,

"Ariya."

2

*H*earing her name, an anxious expression flashed over her face, but then returned to normal as she scanned the room for the speaker. "Who are you? How do you know my name?" She asked as soon as our gazes met.

"Haha." I laughed, thinking she was making a joke. But her tense expression still remained unfazed.

You seriously don't remember me?" I asked again, completely serious this time. "From four years ago?"

After a slight consideration, she slowly shook her head. "Sorry, you must've made a mistake. I don't think I've met you before."

"What do you mean?" I scratched the back of my head frantically, messing up my dark hair even more. Looking into her amethyst eyes, I decided to try my luck again. "The shooting stars?"

She shook her head and said slowly, "No, sorry. Doesn't ring any bells."

"I-If we haven't met before, then why do I know your name?" I asked again, not willing to let this chance pass by.

With all of the commotion us two were causing, I could hear many classmates mutter questions like "Meteor shower of 2016? He was there?"

Before the blond girl had a chance to respond, however, Mr. Eric interrupted us, "I don't know what the heck is going on here, but you can't waste more class time. You two can clarify this after class. We're already five minutes behind schedule."

I sighed and reluctantly nodded. Even though that sparkle of hope only lasted a few seconds, I figured that it was worth chasing for.

"I have no doubt she's Ariya, but why can't she remember me?" I asked myself, clenching my fist tight. *"Although it was four years ago, there's no way she would forget something so important."* I turned around to face the front of the room with a bitter taste in my mouth. *"After literally sacrificing myself to save her, how in the world can she forget that?"* As Mr. Eric began teaching and everyone took out their books, I sneaked a peek at Ariya. Her angelic features still resembled her face of her youth from four years ago. However, oddly enough, I was able to sense that something was missing.

The rest of the morning went by painfully slowly as I constantly found myself glancing at Ariya in every class. Lunch finally rolled around at 12 o'clock. I grabbed my food quickly went over to the seat directly facing Ariya and plopped myself down. "Hey." I said awkwardly.

She looked up from her tray of food and smiled, "What's up?"

"Oh, I'm that guy from this morning. I said I knew you in homeroom." From the way that she casually said "what's up?" I thought she forgot me again.

"Don't worry." She laughed, "I remember you all right."

"Wait! If you remember me, then does that mean…?!" I shouted at the top of my lungs as soon as I reached this conclusion, which made everyone in the room look our way.

"Uh…sorry. If you're still asking about that, my answer is still the same." She shook her head and sighed.

"To be honest, that's what I thought you'd say. Sorry to disturb your lunch, I'll take my leave now." I whispered as I stood up.

"No no, you don't have to." She said and grabbed the sleeve of my shirt quickly, accidentally knocking over her can of orange juice on the table. "In fact, stay here."

Suddenly, I felt someone lightly tap me on my shoulder. When I turned around, I saw a red-head standing in front of me. "What's new, Kai? You're still not giving up on her?" He said mockingly as he sat down next to me.

"Whatever you say, Ben." I shrugged.

He ignored me and turned his attention to Ariya, who had been clearing up the mess on the table until now. "Hey gorgeous. I heard that you're new to this city. How do you like it so far?"

"New to the city?" I thought to myself. *"But she has been here for at least four years since the Shooting Stars… What's he talking about?"* I assumed that Ben was just trying to get the conversation started, but Ariya's response was even more surprising.

"Yeah, my family and I moved here just a couple of weeks ago." She continued after taking a slight pause, "Although my dad is always complaining about how the town we used to live in is more relaxing."

I jerked my body slightly in shock. *"I know for a fact that both of Ariya's parents had died in that accident. So what does she mean by her dad? Is he her foster parent? But what about the fact that she's new to this city? Is she lying about this? But what for? What's she going to get by lying about these things?"* All of these questions floated into my head one by one. Of course, there is no way I could ask all of them in front of everybody without embarrassing her. I had to shake all of them off until later, when I can get her to clarify everything, just the two of us.

My thought was interrupted again by Ben's voice as he spoke to Ariya, "So what do you like to do in your free time? What's your hobby?"

"I don't usually have free time because my parents want me to learn all the school materials ahead of time so I can get good grades." She explained casually, as if her answer was already well-rehearsed beforehand, "But if I finish all of that as well, I would help my parents around in their shop. My family recently rented a house down the street from the school. We're using the front of it as a convenience store."

"Are you serious?" Ben asked, surprised.

"Yeah, why?"

Ben slammed his fist onto the table, "Man! Your parents are tough! They're not even letting you have fun."

"It's all right." Ariya chuckled, waving it off. "It's not their fault. My family isn't as rich as you guys, so we have to work harder than everyone else."

Ben muttered, "Anyway, you wanna hang out together after school? I can show you all of the cool stuff in this city. And there's also an amazing restaurant not far from here!"

"I don't know..." Ariya muttered.

"Ah, come on!" Ben said. "It's only for a couple of hours after school!"

"I guess my parents will be fine with it because it's just this one time." Ariya said. "Oh! Now you just got me excited! "

I don't know why, but that simple exchange between the two caused a big stir within me. I should be happy that my friend, Ben, is getting along with someone. But a feeling of unease consumed me, making my heart ache. *"What do you call this feeling?"*

Before I had a chance to think about the question, Ben poked me on the head. "Yo Kai, you got any plans for the afternoon? You can come too."

"Huh?" I said, confused. "You want me to come with you two?"

"Yeah. What's wrong? We're friends after all, aren't we?" He said slowly, his face slightly red.

"Yeah... we are... but..." I hesitated. *"It'll be awkward if I go. Ariya and Ben like each other, I'll just be a third-wheel, an outsider."*

"Awww, come on, Kai. You should take a break from video games once in a while and actually enjoy the world around you. Trust me, you won't regret it." While I was figuring out how to compete against Ben, he was already past that. From his words and his gestures, I was able to tell that he genuinely wanted his friend to be happy.

I turned my gaze toward Ariya, who was smiling as well. When our eyes met, she said," Yeah, it'll be better if you come too. It's gonna be a blast!"

"Ahh! How bad can it be?!" I said at last "I-if both of you insist... I guess I'll come."

"There we go, Kai!" Ben gave me a pat on the back and said excitedly. "Lunch is almost over now. You got lucky and got put into the same classes as Ariya, so take care of her for me. Let's meet in the central school park after school." And with that sentence, he left me, sitting next to Ariya, wondering what in the world just happened; wondering what it is about him that makes him able to get people to like him so easily.

I decided to stand up and return my lunch tray, and Ariya did the same thing. But neither of us said a word to each other. Then we headed to our classroom in silence. For the three classes in the afternoon, I couldn't concentrate at all. I'd find myself peeking at Ariya with every free second I have. "What have I sunken down to?" I questioned myself, "Stalking someone who I have no chance with."

After the final bell rang, the class let out. Everyone has already returned home, I walked over to Ariya, who was still sitting by her desk. "Ready to go?"

"Give me a second." She said, reaching into her backpack. "I have to pack up and fix my hair. Gotta look nice for Ben."

I tried my best to play it off cool, "Yup! I feel you."

After taking care of everything, Ariya and I were probably the only two people left in the entire building. We slowly strolled across the corridor and down the stairs, neither of us in a hurry. Once we stepped outside, the pleasant warm air and the cloudless blue sky further extended this peaceful scene. Occasionally, a falling orange leaf drifted into view. Even though the school day just ended not long ago, the campus was surprisingly quiet. Eventually, this perfect harmony was interrupted by Ben's shout, who was sitting on a bench in the central school park. "Hey, slowpokes! What's taking you so long? Did Kai mess up on the first day of school and ended up in detention?"

"I'll say this, Ben, surprisingly enough, I rarely get in trouble. The only time I did was when I missed three days of school straight without telling anyone." Ariya stared at me with a suspicious look after my sentence and said to me, "Let's go." Then she lightly jogged to Ben. His flame-colored hair thoroughly blended in with the autumn leaves on the tree behind his back.

"You guys ready?" Ben asked when I got there at last. But without even waiting for our response, he stood up and said, "Let's go to the arcade first."

During our ten-minute walk, I was strolling slightly behind the other two, thinking about what Ariya had said earlier today. If she moved here recently, she certainly knew her way around the city. We were not telling her the directions to get to the arcade, but she was naturally turning at the right intersections as if she has done it one-hundred times before. *"But Ben is too busy flirting with her instead of paying attention to the details."*

Ben suddenly spun around, took me by the hand and yanked me over to him. "What are you doing back there? Get over here!" He yelled.

His words totally caught me off guard and threw me off quite a bit. After taking a few seconds to recover from my initial shock, I said, "Uh...Just thinking about things."

"How lame can you get?" Ben chuckled. "Are still thinking about your video game tournament or whatever?"

"I'm not addicted! Okay?" I tried to defend myself even though I knew my logic wouldn't reach him. But our heated conversation was interrupted by Ariya's laughter. "You look like you two get along so well together!" She exclaimed cheerfully.

"Trust me," I muttered, "It's not as easy as you think."

"Then what do you think about me?" Ben asked with a really even tone.

I didn't want to be put on the spot just like that. Also, I wasn't ready to tell Ben how much I appreciate him as a friend just yet. Especially not in front of Ariya, I'd look like a complete dork. Instead, I changed the conversation and said, "Oh me? I don't know about that, but I think I'll be able to beat both of you in the arcade!" Following that sentence, I dashed into the building with Ben and Ariya chasing right after me.

The arcade was on the first floor of a five-story building. Despite only covering one floor of space, the inside was gigantic and had all sorts of games and machines. Shooting games, board games, and many others, you name it. First, we had to decide on what to play since we have a limited amount of time. However, settling on a game we all agreed on was later proven impossible due to the countless number options to try out. In the end, we concurred on one game per person - The three of us would play the others' favorite. That way, we would only have to play three games, and everyone would also get to play their favorite.

Ben wanted to show off his soccer skills by playing Table Soccer, not realizing that the two basically had no connection whatsoever. Then ended up losing to both Ariya and me.

I decided to display my aiming and shooting skills from all of my video game experience by playing an FPS - First Person Shooter. Although I wasn't used to the joystick on the machine, I did pretty well that round and left the two of them stunned.

Lastly, when it was Ariya's turn, she wanted to have a dancing competition between us three. I was sure both Ben and I would get utterly destroyed in dancing. So we were saved when Ben's mom called and told him to come home. He said, "Sorry guys, but apparently my parents' boss is at my house right now, and I have to go so I can meet him as well."

I could tell Ariya was clearly disappointed, but she tried her best to hide it anyways. "Sure, We already had enough fun. I'm glad we were able to hang out like this."

"Of course." Ben said, "We can spend more time like this together in the future. See you guys tomorrow."

Once Ben walked out of the building, Ariya turned to me and said, "Stop staring."

"Oh right." I quickly mumbled and averted my gaze "Sorry, that wasn't..."

"So what do you want to do right now?" She asked after cutting me off.

"You looked like you wanted to dance. I don't mind waiting for you to hit a few songs." I proposed.

"Really?" She shouted excitedly, her face brightening up. "Trust me, I'll blow your mind away." She suddenly hesitated when she reached into her pocket. "I don't have any money on me..."

"Don't worry." I said, "I have some on me."

"Oh! You're so nice! Thank you, Kai! I'll pay you back tomorrow!" She said as I gave her the coin.

After inserting the money into the machine, she stood on the dance pad and got to work, taking steps with incredible reaction time left and right. Her height was almost as tall as mine. But she was so agile she could've become a gymnast if she wanted to. By the time the song ended, her entire face was red, but she ended up receiving a remarkable ninety-four percent.

"Come on, Kai." Ariya waved at me from the machine, "Come dance with me!"

"But I've never danced before." I complained. "I'm going to mess up horribly if I do."

"I'm the only one who's going to see it, don't worry. I won't say anything bad." She hopped down from the mat and dragged me over. "You're probably not as bad as you think."

After Ariya selected a song, she began to teach me how to dance. How to turn, how to move, and all the technical stuff. And I was starting to get the hang of it after a while. Once the speed of the song accelerated to its peak, I was still able to keep up with the instructions Ariya was shouting at me. Eventually, she got bored teaching and jumped onto the mat next to mine and started to dance with me as well. Even though our skills weren't on the same level, I tried to keep up with her anyways. The tempo of the song was rapid, yet my heart was beating even quicker than that.

"Lucky me… Dancing with the girl I like." I thought to myself with a smile on my face. After the song ended, I checked the scoreboard and saw I got a sixty-eight percent.

"Congratulations!" Said Ariya as we high-fived each other, "You got a passing grade!"

"What do you call this feeling?" I asked myself again as we walked out of the arcade. Once we got outside, the sunset layered an orange drape on our clothes, dyeing them bright red.

"It's been a really enjoyable day." Ariya began, "We can have dinner together sometime in the future. I honestly liked the dancing part the best, too bad Ben missed out on it."

"Yeah, me too. And I wasn't as bad as I thought." I said, "Where's your house? I'll walk you home."

"Oh. You don't have to. I can get there myself. It's all the way down that road." She said, pointing down the street. However, when she did, she caught sight of someone behind a food stand on the sidewalk, selling roasted sweet potato. A wave of yearning flushed over Ariya's face.

"You want some?" I asked, already walking to the stand.

"N-no! I'm fine." She said quickly, embarrassed.

Ignoring her statement, I said to the man selling them "I'll take two, please."

I took the two sweet potatoes, which were fresh out of the oven, and walked back to Ariya."Here you go. Careful, it's hot."

"I-I told you I'm fine." Ariya said slowly at first. "But I'll take it if you already bought it. Thanks!"

She excitedly took the sweet potato from my hand and after fumbling it a few times, blew on it to cool it down. "It smells so good!" I couldn't help but grin at her childish behavior.

"By the way," I said, "My house is in that direction too. Let's go together."

She sighed lightly but nodded. "Sure, I guess that'll work. But please don't show yourself in front of my parents."

"Sure, but why?" I asked.

"Please." She pleaded again. "Just don't."

I knew this must be a sensitive topic for her, so I shrugged and let it slide as we resumed our walk.

Despite all of the traffic surrounding us, it felt like we were the only two people present. "I wish time would just stop itself, so I can enjoy this moment between us to the fullest." I whispered quietly as the light from the sunset faded away.

"Alright! Thanks for walking me home, Kai." Ariya said as we reached the building next to hers. "You can head back to your house now. I'll walk the rest of the way by myself."

"Sure," I said, waving back at her. "See you tomorrow at school!"

Once I was sure I left Ariya's field of vision, I dove into a bush on the side and slowly moved back to her house. I didn't like following people around in secret nor stalking them, but I had to figure out who Ariya has been living with and why she was lying in school.

Night had already fully enveloped the city in darkness. After finding myself a good hiding spot behind a car parked across the street from Ariya's house, I crouched down and saw her just as she entered through the front door of the convenience store. Immediately following that, the only other person in the room, who I assumed was a man because of the tremendous height difference, ran up to her and said something as he slammed the door shut. I couldn't hear their conversation from all the way over where I was standing, but I was able to see most of it through the window. Ariya seemed to be really shaken up. She took a few steps backward, but then was shoved to the ground.

I silently bit my tongue and watched in silence, too shocked to say anything. I wanted to run up and help her, but considering the circumstances, Ariya wouldn't necessarily be in a better position if I helped. When I fixed my eyes back into the store again, I saw the man swinging a bat at Ariya, who was crawling into a ball on the floor. Three swings onto her head, another two onto her shoulders, then another three onto the lower parts of her body. That was the last thing I remembered before I broke into a mad dash back to my house with tears in my eyes.

I woke up forty minutes earlier than usual the next morning because I went to bed so early last night. Even though I didn't eat anything for dinner, I wasn't feeling the least bit of hunger. "What have you gotten yourself into, Ariya?" I whispered as I sat on my bed. "You were so calm and cheery in school and when we were hanging out. You told those lies so we wouldn't worry about you? How? When you know what's going to happen to you when you come home, how can you let all of that go without saying a word to anyone?"

I came downstairs an hour later, surprised to find Mia, still in her pajamas, already up. She sat next to the dining table by herself with no lights on.

"Hi, Mia. You're up early today."

"Yeah! Because of you!" She yelled. "I was worried! You came home yesterday so late, ran straight up into your room, completely ignored me, and didn't even have dinner!"

"Look, I'm sorry." I said slowly. "But a lot of things happened yesterday."

"Yeah? Like what?"

I sighed, "Can we not talk about it? I really don't want to."

Mia took a deep breath, "Fine, I understand. I'm not gonna talk about it anymore. I already made your breakfast, it's on that table." She said, pointing at the kitchen table. "I'm going back to sleep now because I basically didn't get any last night."

"Thanks." I muttered. And before she closed the door to her room, I yelled, "Mia!"

"Yes?"

"I'm really sorry. I know I'm a mess and you shouldn't be taking care of me right now. But... thank you."

"No problem," Mia said slowly, poking her head out from the side of the door. "I'm always here for you."

Breakfast was cake and waffles. I didn't touch the cake but decided to pack it and bring it to school. All I could think about was Ariya. The incident from yesterday night still felt like a really hazy dream.

The first thing I did when I arrived at school was sprint to homeroom, praying that Ariya was okay and at school as usual. But today, the seat that Ariya sat in was empty.

"Where's she?" I asked.

"I'm not supposed to tell you this, but you seemed really anxious when you came in." Mr. Eric answered. "But Ariya's in the hospital right now. She called me last night, saying she had a fever."

"Lying to people again so we won't worry about you? Is that what you want, Ariya?" I asked sarcastically.

"Kai." Mr. Eric said. "Why do you ask?"

"I-It's nothing." I muttered as I returned to my seat. After glancing at Ben a few times, I walked over to him and began, "So I think I should tell you this..."

"I already know." He said, cutting me off. "She called me last night. She had a really high temperature."

"No, that's not it." I whispered.

"What's not it?"

Ignoring Ben, I said "I'm going to visit her in the hospital after school today. You better come too."

"She told me last night that she didn't want us to come." Ben explained. "She's recovering."

"She also told you she had a fever, didn't she? But that's not true at all!" I said, raising my voice. "She wants to see us. She wants to see her friends when she's weak! She needs her friends when she's weak!"

"Who do you think you are, smartypants? Out of all the friends I've had, you are the worst!" Ben shouted, "Did Ariya call you? Did she tell you anything? No, she didn't!"

"That's because I saw the entire thing happen!" I yelled back. I felt all eighteen pairs of eyes in the classroom look our way, but at that moment, I couldn't care less about how I looked in front of everyone else.

Ben slowed himself down after hearing my sentence, "Hold on, you saw what happened?"

"Go visit Ariya with me if you actually care about her." I said, ending the conversation. "And stop trying to act like you know everything. Because you don't."

That was the last time I talked to Ben for the rest of the school day.

Classes went by even more slowly without Ariya in school. I sat in the corner of the cafeteria during lunch so I didn't have to talk to anyone. When school ended at 3:30, I immediately left the campus and headed to the City Hospital, which was the biggest medical center in the urban area. As I was walking, I thought about Ben. He said that Ariya called him last night, which meant that they had each other's phone number. I sighed, *"I still don't have her phone number yet, nor do I have any of her contact information."*

Dark clouds began to pile up in the sky, blocking off most of the sunlight. I arrived at the hospital ten minutes later. The first person I saw was a red-haired teenager standing in the lobby. "Yo, I've been waiting for you." He said,

"So you did come after all."

"Yeah. Hey, Kai," Ben said quietly, his face a little red. "I wanted to say I'm sorry for this morning. I raised my voice and started yelling at you because of something stupid."

"Don't worry about it." I said, patting my friend on the shoulder as I walked past him, making a beeline for the front desk of the hospital. "Let's go see Ariya."

Ben reached out to me with his arm, stopping me at the last second, and said, "I already asked, but they wouldn't tell me her room number. They said Ariya told them to keep any visitors away."

"Well, that was what happened when you tried. But you don't know what will happen to me if I asked, right?" I said,

"No…" Ben muttered. "But I doubt the result will be any different from mine."

I smiled, waving off his concern. "Don't give up so soon, Ben." And continued on.

"How may help you?" The lady at the front desk asked.

"We want to see Ariya. Ariya Clementine. She's our friend. Would you please tell us what room she's in right now?" I asked politely.

"Unfortunately, Miss Clementine still has a high fever right now. As a result, she will not be able to see you. But once her fever recedes, I can tell her that you two boys stopped by to check in on her."

"You shouldn't lie. A fever isn't the reason why she has been hospitalized" I said quietly, clenching my fist. "Also, why can't we see her? We're her friends, and she's in pain right now. Isn't it a friend's duty to help another when they're in trouble?"

"Sir?"

"She has three injuries on her head, and another two on her shoulder, possibly even more. Someone hit her with a bat multiple times last night." I said at last, taking a deep breath after the words left my mouth.

"Woah, woah!" Ben yelled from behind, interrupting me. "How do you know all this?"

"I told you, I saw the whole thing happen." I explained to Ben before turning back to the lady, waiting for her response.

The lady lightly sighed, then said, "Miss Clementine actually knew both of you would come here today. She told me to stop the red-haired one from seeing her. But she also knew that you, the black-haired boy would try to convince me into letting you in." She said, pointing at me. "Ariya is in room 305 on the third floor of the west wing. She has been dreading for you all day. Her family didn't visit her once. Please go and make her feel at ease. It'll help her treatment as well."

"Ariya, we've only been with each other for less than a day… But you already saw through me, and knew what I would've done." I turned to Ben with a smug expression on my face and whispered, "See, what did I tell you? It works when I'm the one asking."

After we thanked the lady at the front desk, we went from the central lobby to the west side of the building. After taking the elevator two floors up, we found room 305 with the name "Ariya Clementine" written on the outside. Before I was about to knock on the door, my hand froze in mid-air, and I sunk into deep thoughts. "I don't think I should see her." I muttered.

"Huh?" Ben asked, confused. "What do you mean?"

"I think it would be best if you two talked in private." I said, Even though I would love to see Ariya right now, it would put me in a really awkward situation.

"That's where you're wrong," said Ben. "You were the one who told me this morning that I had to come and visit Ariya. You were also the one who convinced the lady on the first floor to let us through."

"I know, but still…"

"You were like this yesterday afternoon when you asked you to hang out with us," Ben said. "You were reluctant in the first place too, but you came. What was the result? Wasn't it a blast? Wasn't it fun? So stop worrying about all of the details, and go. After all, isn't a friend's duty to help the other when they're in trouble?"

I gave Ben a bittersweet smile on my face. "You're pretty cruel, Ben. Using my own words against me."

Without warming, an awfully familiar voice shouted from inside the room. "What are you two talking about without me? Get in here!"

I half-heartedly pushed the door open with trembling hands, too afraid to see Ariya in her current condition. Although I knew it was coming, my body still froze in shock when I saw her.

Ariya was sitting on her bed, dressed in a white gown. Her head was wrapped with layers and layers of bandages, drenched red by her own blood. Her arms were covered in bruises. Most importantly, there was a wheelchair right next to her bed.

The window in her room was closed. A bird with feathers the color of flame, however, leaped around the windowsill on the outside to avoid the pouring rain.

Ben dashed over to the side of her bed as soon as we entered her room. "Jesus!" He shuddered. "What happened to you?!"

Ariya's hand instantly flew up to her head, like she was trying to fix her unkempt hair but forgetting her injury. "It's so good to see you! Thanks for coming, Ben," Ariya mumbled, somehow still maintaining her usual fake smile. Then, after an awkwardly long silence, she added, "And you too, Kai. I'm fine. You shouldn't let me distract you from your school work."

Ben said, "It's a Friday. Don't worry about it."

"You still shouldn't be wasting your time. I'm fine."

"Why?" I asked quietly as I gritted my teeth.

"What?"

"How long are you going to pretend? To pretend that you're fine? Look at you right now! You're a mess!" I snapped, "How do you expect us to believe you're fine?"

For the first time, I saw the smile vanish from Ariya. She covered her face with both of her hands and began to sob.

"Come on, Kai. What was that for?" Ben grunted, "Speaking of which, Ariya, who did all of this to you anyway? It couldn't have been your parents, right?"

I was just about to blurt something out when I saw Ariya's distorted face drowning in despair. Her expression was awfully familiar, I felt like I've seen it before, but I couldn't quite put my finger on it.

Then it hit me after a few seconds. The memories rushed back into my mind like a wave. The image in my head was blurry because it was from such a long time ago. I stared into the ceiling and thought to myself, *"How could I ever forget it? That desperate look she had on her face the day her parents died. It was also the day I saved her, four years ago."*

After reminiscing about the past, I walked to the other side of Ariya's bed and knelt down next to her. "Ariya, don't you ever worry about bothering Ben or me. You might not be able to tell, but we actually like to hang around you."

'Yeah, Ariya." Ben added. "If you need something, make sure to let us know."

Ariya slowly lifted her head, her eyes still wet. "Thank you."

Ben asked. "How long are you going to be in the hospital for? A few more days?"

"Yeah," Ariya assured. "It's mainly because of my legs."

"You might actually make it for the school orientation trip in a week." Ben added.

"Orientation trip? What's that?" Ariya asked.

They announced it at school today. The entire freshman class is going to a camp a few hours away for one night." I explained. "It's like a way for classmates to get to know each other better."

Ariya sighed, "But when I get out, I'll have to be in a wheelchair. I won't be able to walk for about another month or two."

"The teachers never said the students can't go in a wheelchair," I smirked. "Either Ben or I will help you get around."

"But then you won't be able to enjoy yourselves then" Ariya muttered.

"Didn't we just tell you? Don't worry about bothering us. In fact, it's not a bother at all!" Ben said before I had the chance to, so I simply nodded at him.

We stayed with Ariya in her room for another hour. We wanted to stay with her longer before leaving, but it was still raining outside so we couldn't go anywhere. For most of that time, Ben was talking to her about the fun things that happened today. I stayed quiet for the entire conversation because my school day wasn't particularly interesting. What Ben didn't mention to Ariya was the fight we had this morning. After a while, the sky began to clear up, and the moon was already making its way into the air.

Before Ben and I left, I walked over to my backpack which I dropped next to the door when we entered the room. I reached into the outer section, took out a plastic box and handed it to Ariya. "Here. It's a slice of cheesecake my sister and I made. It tasted pretty good in my opinion."

Ariya tried to sit up to receive it, forgetting that her legs were injured. "Ouch!" She yelped loudly.

"Be careful," I said, placing the cake on her nightstand next to her bed. "There's a fork in the box, make sure to eat it and tell me what you think."

"Thanks again." Ariya chirped before we walked out the door. "That was really entertaining, talking to you two."

We said goodbye to Ariya for the last time before leaving. Before I shut the door, I got one last good look at her. She was still wearing her fraudulent smile. I silently vowed then, *"Where's that genuine smile of yours from four years ago? I promise, Ariya, I'll help you bring that beautiful part of you back."*

3

After saying goodbye to Ben outside of the hospital, I began to walk back to my house. After the rain, the cool evening temperature was perfect for a stroll. There weren't even a lot of pedestrians on the sidewalk nor were there any traffic blocking the way. I began to whistle lightheartedly, which was something I almost never did because of the constant stress. However, my phone rang a short beep just as I began to whistle a melody. "Huh? Not many people have my number." I murmured as I reached for the phone in my pocket.

The message was sent by an anonymous person, which meant they weren't on my contact list. "How do they have my number? In the first place?" I asked myself.

But one look at the message clarified everything and made me gasp in surprise. It read:

Hey Kai,

Thank you for stopping by with Ben today to see me. That was really nice of you, and I enjoyed it a lot. Your cheesecake was really delicious, I ate it in three gulps. I hope you can make more for me in the future!

Can you guys come to visit me tomorrow after school as well? It gets pretty boring when I'm stuck in a hospital room all day.
P.S. Can you buy some donuts along with the cake for me? I know I'm asking for a lot, but please.

Thank you!

After I finished reading this message, my hand was shaking with excitement. *"Why is my heart racing?"* I asked myself. *"What do you call this feeling again?"*

I didn't know the answer to my own question then, but I had a feeling that I was on the right track. "Just like everything else, there's gotta be a start, right?" I said to myself as I sprinted all the way home.

"Where have you been, Kai? You're late again." Mia yelled, "Oh? You're in a good mood today."

"I was visiting a friend." I said, taking off my shoes.

"Was it Ben?" Mia asked.

"Nah. It was someone else. She's in the hospital right now."

Mia's eyes lit up for a second and she yelled, "Oh! It's a girl!"

I sighed, all of the excitement from before seemed to tumble onto the ground. "It's not what you think. I don't have a chance with her."

As I walked over to the kitchen for dinner, I thought to myself, *"If I don't have a chance with Ariya, then why am I still chasing after her?"*

"Why don't you have a chance with her?"

I didn't even want to answer that question, but I knew I had to face it. "She likes my best friend."

"Oh." Mia muttered quietly, "That's gotta be tough."

"Hey Mia?" I said suddenly.

"Yeah?"

"Do you know any places around here that sell donuts? Ariya asked me to buy some for her."

I bit into a slice of steak Mia made for me while I waited for her response. Normally, I would've exclaimed how great its taste was. But perhaps something else was bothering me, I only nodded instead.

"Ariya." Mia said the name aloud. "That's nice. From what you're doing right now, it looks like you haven't given up on her yet. And since she's in the hospital, it seems that you're the one taking care of her, not Ben."

"I guess."

"The convenience store a few blocks away finally has donuts. It seems that the new owner is loading up on junk food." Mia said. "But they close at nine so you should hurry up if you want to buy them tonight."

Mia started talking about how her day went for the rest of dinner. She went to a friend's house and they had lunch together. I, however, couldn't pay attention to her story because my mind floated elsewhere. After the meal, she took the dishes into the sink and I headed outside to the convenience store around eight thirty.

There were only a few streetlights on the road my house is on. But once I crossed over to the main street, more cars and traffic were coming into view. The store was only a few blocks away, which should've only taken me about ten minutes, but I walked extra slowly and sometimes even stopped and stared up at the starry night in awe. It wasn't until I was already in front of the shop when I noticed how awfully familiar this building looked. It took me a few seconds to realise that this was the store Ariya lived in, also the one she got hurt in.

I stopped on the front doorsteps, about to turn back. Seeing Ariya injured so badly is already making me feel horrible. I couldn't imagine how I would feel if I actually went in.

"But I can find out who the person was. And perhaps more things about the incident. Plus, I came here to buy food for Ariya, didn't I?" I thought to myself. Finally, after about a minute of deep breaths, I worked out the courage and pushed open the front door.

"Hello?" I shouted. Only to find no answer.

I rang the bell next to the entrance, but there seemed to be no response to that either. *"Maybe the owner will show up when I checkout at the counter."* When I started to walk around the shop, looking for donuts, cakes, and other sweets, something caught my eye. It was a girl's high school uniform, hanging on the wall behind the checkout sign. I would've simply ignored it if it was a normal piece of clothing. But this one had a yellow stain on the right sleeve. It was from yesterday, during lunch, when Ariya tried to get me to stay at her table she bumped over the can of orange juice.

Suddenly, someone shouted, "Give me a second, I'll be with you shortly." The voice sent a chill down my spine. Shortly after that, a really tall and large man in his forties stepped out of the door behind the counter. He wore a white T-shirt and shorts. "Are you here to shop or not? We're going to close soon."

"Uh… Yeah. Do you sell any donuts?" I asked quietly, a little bit afraid.

"Yeah, we do… Wait." The man said abruptly, his eyes squinting as he stared at me. "You're...."

"Sorry?"

"You're Kai, aren't you?"

"How do you know me?" I immediately took a step back and asked.

"I saw you on the high school's registration website because you are Ariya are in the same class, and I heard her talking about you a few times."

I took a deep breath and tried not to sound shocked, "Are you Ariya's father?"

"Yeah," He said after a slight pause, "I am. But if you're looking for her, then tough luck. She had a fever and is in the hospital right now."

Of course, I could've jumped at his statement and proved him wrong. But I also saw this as an opportunity. If he isn't conscious of the fact that I've been with Ariya, I could try to approach him and see if I can get some of my questions answered. Before I could've said anything, however, he opened his mouth.

"Listen, kid. I just wanted to say thanks."

"Huh?" I wasn't sure if I heard him right. How could the man who beat Ariya up know to appreciate someone?

"You know how she told you she recently just moved here?"

"Y-Yeah?"

"Well, what she said wasn't true. It's just an excuse. Ariya has been living in this city for her entire life except for when she was twelve. She was taken away for something regarding the Meteors. When she came back, however, she wasn't as well-mannered as she is right now. She has been made fun of and laughed at because of how problematic she was as a kid. Ariya said she has only met one person that mattered to her in her entire life, and that was a long time ago."

From the moment I walked into the store, I thought the storeowner was a violent and uncultured man who would beat anyone up if they didn't listen to him. So when he told me everything, including the truth Ariya was hiding, I was really surprised. Lastly, this person he was talking about, the one mattered to Ariya the most, I promised myself I'd one day make her care about me the same way.

"T-thanks for telling me all of this… Wait…" As If suddenly realizing I've been missing something important, I shouted, "Wait! Three years ago? Then it's the same time as me!"

The man stared at me with a questioning gaze, "The same as you? What are you talking about?"

"Oh, I meant… uh… nevermind."

"Uh-huh." He shrugged.

I decided to bring the conversation back to where we started, "Why was she lying to me then?"

He stood silently and considered it for a second, "She probably wanted to become your friend. She thought if she told you the truth, you wouldn't want to befriend her anymore."

"I like Ariya because of who she is right now, not because of who she was years ago." It felt weird to say it. However, I was glad I did, because I was able to convey my feelings to someone else.

"So yeah, I just wanted to thank you for being the first person to want to be friends with her. Ariya's mood has been lighter lately, because of you."

"What about the other kid, Ben? Did Ariya say anything about him?" I asked.

"Oh yeah, I know him." The man answered, scratching his mustache. "Ariya likes him too, she talked about him a few times too."

I silently nodded, still not believing my ears nor my eyes. This was the man who physically assaulted Ariya, now he's treating me like I was his best friend.

"Thanks for telling me all of this, I really appreciate it." I said at last.

"Uh… just don't tell her about any of this. This conversation stays between us two, okay?"

I smirked, "Sure thing."

After that, I picked out a cake and some other snacks off the shelves. The man didn't even charge me anything, saying it was a gift for the friend of his daughter. When I left the store and was on my way home, my phone rang with a "Ding!", for receiving a text message. At first I thought it was from Mia, asking what was taking me so long, so I was pretty shocked to find out it was from Ben. In the text, he asked me if I wanted to hang out with him tomorrow morning, and said to meet in front of the city hall at nine if I agree to it.

"When was the last time the two of us hung out together?" I asked myself. *"It's been ages."*

Planning ahead, since it's a Saturday, I was going to spend the morning with Ben and head over to the hospital to Ariya for the afternoon. I replied Ben a "Sure" without an extra thought, wondering what he has in mind for us to do. "Tomorrow is going to be an interesting day!" I shouted as I quickly jogged back home with a smile on my face.

When I woke up the next morning, I was a little annoyed at why Ben chose such an early time for us because I was hoping to get some extra sleep on weekends. But at the same time, I didn't want our hangout to drag out for too long because I didn't want to be late to visit Ariya.

After washing up and getting dressed in a grey tracksuit, I saw the time and quickly hurried downstairs. Mia was still sleeping because she stayed up late and I knew she wouldn't wake up until noon. I scribbled a note for her on the kitchen table and grabbed a sandwich. Then I was on my way.

The walk was relatively peaceful since there were a lot less people in the streets on a saturday morning than there usually would be on weekdays. Unlike yesterday, the sky was sunny and without a single cloud. Some of the leaves on the trees along the sidewalk were already starting to turn yellow as the season progressed. When I arrived at the square in front of the huge glass building, Ben was waiting for me, but he was dressed differently and weirdly.

"Yo." He waved.

"Sorry I'm a little late. Did I make you wait?" I could already see the beads of sweat on his forehead, suggesting how long he was there for.

"Not at all." He answered, waving it off.

"Why are you wearing your… soccer jersey?"

"Do you like it?" He asked, "Uh… I haven't done my laundry in a while, so this is like the only clean shirt I have at the moment."

"The yellow color is super flashy." I commented. "Sooo… what's our plan?"

Ben asked, barely hiding a smile, "Do you know what day is it?"

"Uh… September the ninth?"

"Yes, and no. You dummy! Two years ago today, was the day when I first met you."

My entire body shook with no apparent reason. It might've been the volume he was yelling at me with, or maybe because it was simply the fact that today was our two-year friendship anniversary. I never particularly wanted to search my mind for what happened today two years ago. But as soon as I heard those words, those memories rushed back to me like a wave.

A soccer field next to the City Hall building.

It was a Sunday afternoon, September 9th, 2018. Two weeks after I came back from the secret facility. Because I was absent for an entire year, I wasn't as physically capable as everyone else. And I was known throughout the neighborhood as a clueless, problem child, and even my own mother wasn't an exception. She was around more often back then, but she too thought I was hopeless.

Everyone in my class was invited to play in a soccer match the day before sixth grade started. Back then, the family organizing the game probably didn't even want to invite me. But they felt it would've been an obvious prejudice. Once all twenty-two kids arrived on the field, we had to do my most hated activity of all - splitting into teams.

Just from my half a month of experience since returning, I got left out every single time in situations like this. I played it off cool every time, saying "I don't want to play anyways" as I walked to the corner and sat myself down. I sat there alone, hugging my knees and covering my hurt feelings. Oh! How I wished every time someone would walk up to me and lend me a helping hand. But on that day, a person did. It was a boy in my class wearing a yellow soccer jersey.

"You okay?" The red-haired boy asked, his hand lightly patting my back.

"Y-yeah… I guess."

"You want to play, don't you, Kai?"

I was really surprised to hear him say my name. It's not because how he came to know the information, it's why he paid any attention to it. "You know my name?" I asked.

"Why wouldn't I? You might be introverted and don't like soccer, but there are plenty of things you're good at, right?"

The afternoon sunlight made its way through the orange leaves of the trees. I raised my hand to block the light being shot directly at my eyes, but the boy's hand caught mine at the perfect moment, pulling me off the ground. "Yeah…" I finally answered after a long pause. "There are loads of other things I like."

"Perfect! I just moved here about a week ago. My family is still settling down. Can you show me around the area this afternoon?"

"Y-you want me?" I asked as if not believing my ears.

"Yeah! Why? Are you going to decline?"

I smiled, as if my body suddenly got filled with energy, "No, of course not. I'd love to." It was my first genuine smile in many years.

"Great!" He yelled, his fire-colored hair dancing in the wind as he dashed back onto the field. "Come join us! We need you for the game."

Everything that just happened to me was making my head spin. I ran and caught up to him, "Um... What's your name?" I asked.

He spun around swiftly, holding out his right hand for a handshake. "It's Ben."

I ended up playing horribly that soccer match because I've only played the sport a few times before. While everyone else was making fun of me, Ben would always take me aside, comfort me, and teach me a few tips. There were so many times when I wanted to tell him to stop being nice to me and treat me like everyone else did. But every time I look up at him, I always see the same, honest smile on his face. Its warmth was beginning to melt my frozen heart.

After the soccer match, like I promised, we strolled around town for a little while and I showed him some cool places. We walked and talked until it got dark. It was as if we could never get bored talking to each other.

I invited him to my house for dinner. When we walked into the building, the look on my mother's face was something I'd never forget. At first, she asked me who Ben was. I answered, "A friend." But she almost burst out laughing in response, her face was saying, "How in the world can a person like you make a friend?" Ben, however, surprised me by standing up and speaking for me. He said how good of a person and how nice of a friend I was.

Despite My friend helping me, my mother still didn't believe us. She thought I met him through the internet and the only reason I was talking to him was because we played the same video game, which is also not true. I was about to give up when Ben said something I could never forget.

"Excuse me, ma'am. Why are you doubting Kai so much?" Ben said to my mom with a tone that was neither too harsh nor too easy. It wasn't as soft as a little kid's whining, while it wasn't as harsh as an adult's lecture either. "Your son, Kai, was the first person in this city willing to waste a few hours of his time and show me around the place. If that's not what friends do for each other, then I don't know what is."

It was perhaps my mother's first time hearing a kid say something so mature. As a result, she was incredibly shocked, and I was too. Everytime he said something, Ben's firm voice was able to find the bull's eye.

*Soon after talking to him, my mother's opinion on us changed
dramatically. We hung out every day after school. We'd go to the arcade or
kick the soccer ball around. This continued for about a month or two, until
my mother had to travel overseas for her job and left Mia and I to ourselves
so I had to help out around the house. I've been looking for an opportunity
to thank Ben for changing my life, but I still haven't done it in all these
years.*

At first, I heard a quiet whisper in my ear. Then. after a few
seconds, the sound grew louder and louder. It was a voice, yelling
my name. "Kai! Kai!" I felt a hand on my shoulder. With a pull, it
brought me back to reality.

"Huh?' I muttered, rubbing my eyes.

"What were you doing, Kai? Just blanking out all of a
sudden!" Someone yelled next to me.

When I turned around, seeing his iconic red-colored hair
brought an immediate smile to my face. "H-heh… Sorry about that. I
was thinking about the day you and I met."

"Oh?" He muttered, "That's nice. From the smile you have
one right now, I'm assuming it was some fond memories."

"Yeah." I couldn't help but to steal a peek at him. I thought
he would be smirking as he thought about the first time when he
helped me. Instead, he was drooping his face, staring at the
pavement as we walked. His mood was completely different from
when we just met up five minutes ago. "What's wrong?" I asked.

"It's nothing. Don't worry about it."

I sighed, hoping to change the topic to something cheerful. I
didn't want our first hangout in half a year to be a bust. "Sooo…" I
started, "How's soccer going for you?"

"Average." Ben said simply.

"Any interesting things happen at practice?" I asked again.
"When's your first game of the season."

"Practice was normal. Our first game is this afternoon."

"Oh? This afternoon!" My eyes lit up as I raised my voice, "
Why didn't you tell me earlier?"

"Not like the match is gonna matter once I le-" Ben jerked
his body without warning and his voice came to an abrupt end,
leaving the sentence hanging in the air, unfinished.

"Once you what?"

However, this time, he didn't give me a response. He probably didn't even hear my question. Ben just kept his head down and continued to walk forward. I kind of sensed this was related to the topic he told me to not worry about just a few minutes before and decided to keep quiet.

We reached the end of the street in silence. I patiently waited for Ben to come back to his consciousness. Eventually, he looked up at me and muttered, "Sorry for being such a crappy friend today."

"Don't worry about it. People have bad days. We can call it for today if you want. There will always be more time later."

"I don't know…"

"You don't have to feel bad about it."

Ben averted his gaze and looked away from me, glancing at the surrounding shops and people. He closed his eyes and gave himself a slight nod. Then, with his eyes lighting up, he shouted, "Let's get a drink at the store over there!"

"Uh...sure." I was a little taken back by his sudden change in attitude, considering how he was sulking just moments earlier. We turned right at the end of the street we were on, and strolled toward the beverage store.

"Do you know what my parents' jobs are?" Ben spoke up all of a sudden, shattering the silence around us.

"No, I never asked you, so you never told me."

"Okay. Then I'll tell you now." Ben took a deep breath and began, "Ever since I was born, my mom and dad had been part of the information department of a huge computer business. Their job was to travel around the country and sometimes even the world to find out which markets are prospering and which are not in order to help their company's selling routine. Everytime my parents move to different areas, it's usually for a long period of time. As a result, I have to go with them."

During his long rant, I didn't say a single word to interrupt him. Ben took a slight pause and sighed, " I have already moved to five different cities in the country, and every time I do, I hated the experience so much! Sure, for the previous three times when we moved, I was really little and didn't remember much. But the last time we moved, the fourth time, was extremely painful. It was a regular school day, and I was in fifth grade. After parting with my best friend, Ted, I returned to my home in the afternoon, only to find everything in our apartment gone. Everything was packed, and there were four huge suitcases lying on the floor. At first, I didn't know what was going on, but then I realized I've been in situations like this before. In fact, this scene was so familiar I knew what was going to happen: I would break into tears and start to complain about moving. But what could I do? My mom would always comfort me by buying me a few toys. And in just one day, I would find myself attending a brand new school with a room of complete strangers. I got a text from Teddy two days later, asking me why I wasn't at school. I couldn't even respond to him when I realized I never even said goodbye. I had to leave everyone behind and start everything from zero. I felt like I didn't have a permanent home, everywhere was temporary. I want to have someone I can rely on, at least for a while! And you! You were that someone, Kai! But now… I have to… I don't want to go through all of this again!"

I was staring at the ground up until Ben finished. His eyes were wet with tears when I finally looked up at him. Before I had a chance to comfort him, he took off running and left me behind. And just like that, our time together today ended as abruptly as it began.

I stood outside the door of Ariya's room in the hospital with two bags of groceries, one I brought from the shop and the other one from home. After knocking on the door, Ariya responded quickly, "Come in!"

"Hey." I said as I pushed open the door. "How are you doing?"

"Pretty good." Ariya answered with her normal smile, laying in bed in her regular patient's clothes. Her hair draped loosely on both sides of her face. But her bandage wrapped around her head today was clean so I could see she was no longer bleeding. "It's just you?" She asked as she peeked through the door.

"Uh… yea." I answered, a little taken back, "Ben's at a soccer match. Did you want to see him?"

"Nah, it's good just the two of us."

I nodded and reached down into one of the bags, "Here's the cake you wanted."

"Oh my Gosh!" She exclaimed, her eyes lit up as she immediately reached for a slice, "Thanks so much!"

"Don't worry about it."I smiled as I sat in the chair next to her bed, setting the bags aside, "Did anything interesting happen in the past day?"

"What interesting things could've possibly happened?" She asked sarcastically. "All I do is sit here and read books and think about fun stuff."

"You can't even go outside?" I asked as I stared out the window. There was a clear view of the beautiful blue sky from where I was standing. Moreover, perhaps it was because of the weather difference, but the mood of the room felt a lot lighter than yesterday.

"Of course not." Ariya replies, sounding irritated. "I obviously can't go anywhere by myself. Also I'm not the only person the nurses have to take care of. They're not going to waste an hour of their time just for me."

"Where do you want to go?" I asked.

"Huh?"

"I'll take you. Where do you want to go?"

"Oh really? You don't have to. I only wanted to have more of that cake because of how bad the food here is."

I said smirking as I shot her a thumbs up, "Then let's fill you up at a good restaurant. And for the one millionth time, don't worry about bothering me."

Ariya sat on her bed, her hand rubbing against her chin as if in deep contemplation. Finally, she lifted up her face and grinned, "If you want it that much, then I'll go out with you tonight."

"Oh." I was a little taken back and paused, my face awkwardly blushing. "I wouldn't call it going out with you…"

Ariya lowered her voice even though there was no other person in the room. She whispered into my ears, "Just once, tonight."

"Uh…" I tried to get the words out of my mouth. I wanted to accept her offer more than anything in the world. But I didn't know why I couldn't say anything.

"Well?" Ariya asked again. Although her body was covered in bruises, she tilted her head and smirked. "You unsocial person who can't get a single girl to like him, do you want to go out with me?"

What was I waiting for? I closed my eyes slowly, putting everything aside, throwing away all concerns, I lifted up my hand and placed it on top of her's on the bed, "Of course. I'll go out with you."

"Now that's more like it. I'm gonna change my clothes because I look like a mess right now." But her hand soon snapped away from mine, "What are you doing touching my hand like that all of a sudden?"

"What? I was just being nice." I muttered, slightly blushing at the awkward gesture.

"Whatever, we're going out for dinner anyways." She pointed at a hair tie on the table, "Can you get that for me?"

I walked over and picked it up. It had almost the same color as Ariya's amethyst eyes, only slightly darker. Instead of giving it to her, however, I walked behind her and began wrapping her hair. As soon asI touched it, I was amazed by how soft and flowy Ariya's hair was.

"What are you doing?" Ariya snapped her head around, startled.

"What do you think?" I asked sarcastically as I gathered the hair into my hand and lifted it up. "I'm fixing your hair for you."

A doubtful expression formed on her face. She tilted her head and said, "May I ask how do you know?"

"I used to help my little sister out." I replied as I skillfully wrapped the hair tie around. "There, all done."

"Speaking of which, I heard you mention her before, but how old is your sister? What's her name?"

"Her name's Mia and she's thirteen." I answered, "We're not related by blood. She was adopted into my family a long time ago."

"You're lucky you at least have a sibling." Ariya said quietly. "I wish I had a little brother or sister. It would be nice to have someone keep me company constantly."

"Trust me," I joked, "it's not all bread and butter. They get really annoying."

"They do?" Ariya asked, lifting an eyebrow.

"Yeah. Because our parents are barely here with us, once when I was teaching her how to cook, she messed up so many times I wanted to give up. But at the end of the day… " Even though those were frustrating times, recollecting those memories brought a smile to my face. "At the end of the day," I continued, "She's family. And family doesn't give up on each other."

"Family…" She was staring at the wall of her room with an empty gaze. A faint wave of cloudiness flashed over her eyes as she muttered the word silently, but it soon disappeared into nothingness.

I had a faint idea of what she might have been thinking. With the slightest hope, I thought there was a chance that she finally remembered me and what happened that day four years ago, "What's wrong?"

"I was just thinking about… N-nothing." She shook her head slowly. "Are you ready to leave?"

"Sure." I nodded, "Are you ready?"

"I can't change my pants because of my legs. But I'll change my shirt."

"Sounds good. I'll just wait outside." I said, making my way to the door. "Give me a shout when you're done."

There was a bench facing Ariya's room just outside in the dark hallway. I sat there clenching my fist, frustrated about how she came to the topic of what happened four years ago but she wasn't able to recall what truly happened even once. Then, I thought about what the storeowner said about Ariya being taken away the year after the Meteors. *"Taken away. To where though?"* I was almost certain he meant to one of the research centers similar to the one I was in, but I still groaned at the fact I wasn't able to clarify with him earlier.

Out of the blue, a loud shriek followed by a metallic noise coming inside Ariya's room brought me back to reality. "Ariya!" I instantly leaped out of my seat as if I had a launch pad behind me and dashed toward her door, "Are you okay!?"

"T-the wheelchair!" She screamed, "I fell! Please come in!"

I tried turning the doorknob multiple times, only to find it locked. "It's not working!" I pounded on the door many times, in vain.

"Kai! My legs are getting crushed under the wheelchair! I c-can't move! Please help!"

"I'm trying! Watch out, I'm going to knock the door down!" I took a few steps back and charged at the door as fast as I could, and collided directly with my right shoulder. Fortunately, t   he door toppled over and I was able to make my way into the room. When I saw Ariya struggling on the floor, I forgot about everything and rushed next to her to lift the wheelchair off, knocking away a chair along the way. "What happened?" I finally asked when everything was done.

Instead of answering me, however, Ariya buried her face in her hands and started to sob. I knelt down next to her and patted her lightly on the back. "I'm sorry I wasn't able to get here faster."

With a teary voice, Ariya said, "I almost thought I lost them."

"Lost what?"

"M-my doctor said i-if I damage my legs one more time before they recover, they will be permanently shattered." She reached down to them, her right hand brushing against the bandages and cast. "I can still feel them… I think they're safe… I think I'm safe."

"That's good…" I nodded, feeling relieved as well.

"Thank you, Kai, for saving my life."

Perhaps Ariya didn't realize how smoothly that sentence flew out of her mouth. But I remembered it very clearly. Four years ago, in the middle of the Meteors, she said those same exact words to me.

"Don't worry about it." I said quietly, waving her off. "How did this happen anyway?"

"I tried to use my arms to help me get to the closet. After I got changed, my arms gave way and I fell onto the side of the wheelchair." Ariya still had her face covered by her hands, so half of her mumbling was barely audible to me.

"If this happens again, don't hesitate to tell me. I'll get to you as fast as I can."

"I-I thought about asking you." Ariya said with a trembling voice, shaking her head, "But you're already doing so much for me… I didn't want to look like such a loser by asking you for help on so many things. Because of how useless I am, you can't even enjoy your Saturday like a normal person."

I reached into my pocket and handed her a tissue. "That's not true. I'm helping you because—"

Pausing my sentence, I realized I've been taking Ariya's situation too easily. After giving it a deeper thought, I realized she could've just lost the ability to walk for her entire life. She would've have to sit on a wheelchair and rely on someone to push her around. I didn't want to give Ariya too much pressure by constantly talking, so all I did was to sit beside her against the side of the bed in silence, looking up at the ceiling once in a while..

Through the clear window, the sun was just about to set, dyeing the sky with a hint of orange. We were sitting by ourselves in Ariya's room until a nurse came to check in on her and saw the mess we made. I did all of the explaining for Ariya because I knew how terrible she must be feeling at the moment. She stayed next to me the entire time, hugging my arm. By the time everything was clarified, Ariya's didn't even notice it herself, but her fingers were already tightly grasping the palm of my hand.

4

*S*oon after the disaster in Ariya's room was taken care of, she checked in with her doctor and she was excused to go to dinner with me.

I slowly and carefully pushed her in and out of the elevator. When we exited the building, we were welcomed by a gust of cool autumn wind. Ariya took a deep breath and chirped, "Fresh air feels so nice! You never realize how important something is until you lose it!"

I nodded in agreement, "I don't know why, but I think I understand what you mean."

"You're weird sometimes." Ariya turned around to look at me with a pout. "How does that even work?"

"It's just a feeling." I shrugged.

Ariya shook her head a few times as if giving up, and asked, "So where are we going?"

I pointed at the second to last building down the street, "You see that circular building? They have some good food in there."

"Oh, that one? Isn't that's one of the nicest restaurants in the city?! Why are we going there? We could've just gone to any other restaurant!"

"Don't worry about it." I said quietly. "It's the first time we're going out for dinner, after all."

As we strolled down the sidewalk quietly and slowly, none of us said a single word to each other. Unlike that time when we were in school, our silence this time, however, wasn't because of awkwardness or the lack of a common topic. It was because both of us wanted to to enjoy this serenity between us two to the fullest. Above, the blue sky revealed a faint trace of the sunset. Either of us would occasionally hum a few tones to accompany the melody of the dancing wind.

Ariya's gaze would sometimes drift off into the stores along the sides of the street. Occasionally an expression of yearning would flash over her face. Every time I asked if she wanted to check something out in the shops, she'd decline my offer. But in the end, when I took her into one, her reaction was as if she had just entered her paradise. We stopped by four shops in total. Because Ariya couldn't move her lower body, she wasn't able to buy any pants or skirts. As a result, she only bought a grey T-shirt and a white shirt. One with the picture of a kitten sewn at the front and the other one had a heart sign with the words "I love you".

"What do you call this feeling?" I asked myself in the gentle wind, my fingers playfully tapping Ariya's shoulders as we wrapped up the shopping and continued to the restaurant. *"Walking with the girl I like in the sunset. As if everything around all disappeared, as if we were the only two people in the entire world."*

When we got to the restaurant at last, it was already thirty minutes later than planned, but it did not stop us from taking our time and enjoying everything. The inner part of the building was heavily decorated with western paintings and artworks. The atmosphere was dim, but the candle on top of every table and the jazz music playing in the background brought the entire setting to life.

The waiter came to our table with the menu and a loaf of bread as starters, he recommended us to have the "Couple's dinner", which led to an awkward moment and I had to explain we were simply classmates and friends. The waiter smiled at our funny reaction and winked at me before leaving.

Sitting in the wheelchair directly across the table from me, Ariya's eyes would sometimes light up as she glanced down the menu. She exclaimed, "It has been ages since I've seen a menu this good... but these price tags though."

"Don't worry about the money." I said, tapping my wallet, "I have plenty."

I sat in my chair without saying a word, a little bit nervous. The waiter came to check in on us after a while and we placed our orders - some steamed lobster for me and a piece of steak for Ariya.

Before coming here, I thought it would be pretty easy for us to get into a conversation, but it turned out to be a lot harder than expected. As we waited for our food, I couldn't think of anything to talk about, so all I could do was to sit in silence and sometimes cast a nervous glance at Ariya. Eventually, she was the one to shatter the silence, "So... what do you want to chat about? We gotta make this dinner enjoyable."

"Gee...I don't know..." I shrugged as I randomly chose a topic to talk about, "How was your summer vacation?"

"It was mostly packed with homework." Ariya answered, "Although I did attend a summer camp for two weeks."

"Oh? What type of camp?" I asked.

"Regular day camp." Ariya said, "They had a lot of fun courses and activities for us to try out. I ended up doing Geography, Astronomy, and sports. It was all really fun!"

"Astronomy? That sounds fancy. What did you learn in it?"

Thinking about it made Ariya chuckle. She said, "To be honest, I didn't really learn anything useful. But a lot of the experiments and projects were really fun though."

"That's nice. Sounds like it was a blast!"

"It was! It really was! What about you, Kai?" Ariya asked, "What did you do this summer? Anything interesting?"

"It's certainly not as fun as yours…" I muttered, my mood and voice suddenly plummeting down into a pit. "I spent most of my time indoors playing games."

"What did I expect?" Ariya joked. "You gotta get outside more, Kai. If we aren't eating together right now, would you still be in your room on your computer?"

"Surprisingly, I didn't even touch my computer once since school started."

"See? You're almost there. The internet isn't everything. The outside world is interesting too."

I nodded in agreement. I've always wanted to thank Ariya for that. Ever since classes began, I met Ariya and everything had been centered around her. I didn't have time to go on the computer nor do I want to because she made my world colorful again.

"What's wrong, Kai? You look pretty sad right now. Don't you like spending time with me?" Ariya asked as she pushed my glass of water closer to me.

"I do… I like talking to you…just hearing you say one word makes my heart race. We had a good time on our way over here too. But this time… I don't know why…"

Before I could say anything else, the waiter came to our table with our food. Ariya and I quietly waited as he gave each of us our plates. When he finally left, Ariya started by saying, "I'm at fault too. I can't even move without you helping me… Like you said before, you haven't had the chance to go on your computer yet because you have to be around me."

"That's not-" I interrupted.

"It is." Ariya continued, ignoring me. "Your life was perfectly fine until I came along. Look at how many hours you've spent with me in the past two days. I'm taking everything away from you because of my uselessness… so why are you still helping me?" Is

"Why am I helping her?" That question somehow sounded really familiar to me. It took me a while to realize it, but once I did, it rang a bell in my head. That day when I saved Ariya during the Meteors four years ago, it was the same question puzzling my mind. And now, here I am, four years later, I'm still not sure if I found the answer yet.

"Come on, let's eat. We don't want the food to get cold." I suggested, pointing at the plates on the table.

"Oh yeah. I haven't heard you talk about your parents yet? What do they do?" Ariya asked as she picked up her fork.

I sighed, "My mom works for a tech company. She travels to places very far away quite often. So I only get to see her once or twice a year."

Ariya nodded, "What about your dad?"

"He…" I said slowly, shutting my eyes, "He died in the Meteors of 2016."

"The Meteors of 2016…" Ariya repeated, sounding each syllable out carefully. Then without warning, Ariya's arms swung upwards and tightly clenched her head. "Ahhh!" She yelled.

"Ariya!" I shouted as I jumped out of my chair and hurried next to her, "What's wrong?"

She wasn't able to give me a clear response. Her hands were still grasping her head, continuing to groan. From the distorted expression she had on her face, I could tell the agony she was in. I brought her head close to my chest, trying my best to make her feel warmer and safer. Eventually, after the pain receded a little bit, I was able to decipher a few words she was saying: "Meteors… parents…die." Then after a pause, she said, "My parents…"

Even though it pained my heart to see Ariya suffering, it was her last sentence that caught my attention. Through those mere five words, lied the sentence I've been waiting for Ariya to say. As she continued to moan, clutching my chest tight, my heart was split into two parts: half sympathetic, half relieved.

The painful headache Ariya was experiencing ended up receding within a few minutes and she was able to recover by herself. I suggested her to return to the hospital, claiming what we went through this afternoon and night was too much to a person who was still sick. Ariya, however, shot my offer down right away. She said she wanted our first dinner together would be a complete one and there was no way she was going to let that go. Every time when we weren't talking or when she was eating, her face would be frowning both in pain and in desperation. But when I said something or when we held a conversation, she would force that frown on her face into a laugh.

I sighed and whispered to myself, *"There's that fake smile again. I promised that I'd get her genuine smile back and never have to see the feint… but here I am, looking at it again."*

I tried to smile back in return, only this one had a bitter taste in it, which led me to think about how many of the dark and twisted things Ariya must have been through in order to put on such an act so many times.

Most importantly, even though she was able to uncover a little bit of her memory about the Meteors, she wasn't able to remember anything more. I tried to get her closer to the answer by asking some questions, "Remember a few minutes ago you yelled your parents and the Meteors a few minutes ago?"

"Yeah." She muttered quietly.

"What made you say that? Did you think of something in the past?"

Ariya locked her brows tight, and sat in her wheelchair quietly as we finished eating. After almost a minute of thinking, she muttered. "I-I can't… The memories… they're so distant."

I let out a deep sigh. When I pushed Ariya out of the restaurant, my hope, like the little candle on the table, flickered out into darkness.

This dream of mine has been shut down so many times before, so I wasn't surprised when I realized it was going to happen again. We got on the sidewalk and strolled slowly under the shimmering moonlight. Both Ariya and I were in silence. After a few minutes, she suddenly surprised me by saying something that I've been waiting to hear for so long.

"But I know something was there in the past, a part of me I have forgotten. I've been missing it all this time."

After taking Ariya back to her hospital room, which was a new one because they had to fix her old room with the broken door, she apologized again about ruining my day. I tried to say it wasn't her fault, but I'm sure those words entered her left ear and went out of the right.

Before I left, Ariya said she couldn't see me tomorrow because she had to take a physical examination. I nodded as I walked through the door and waved her goodnight. The last thing I saw was, again, the phony smile on her face.

By the time I got back to my house, it was already nine thirty; so I knew Mia was going to be mad at me again for coming home so late. But when I rang the doorbell, I heard a trail of rapid footsteps coming closer. Mia, dresses in a white skirt, leaped out of the front door and flew directly into my arms. "Mia!?" I yelled, "What're you doing? What's wrong?"

"Kai..." She sniffled, "Where have you been lately... you haven't even properly talked to me once since school started for you."

"Oh. Have I?" I circled my arms around her body and lifted her up. "I'm sorry. I've been caught up in some other things."

"Don't leave me... like what my parents did... like what your parents did... Kai! Please stay with me!" With unstoppable emotions flowing out of her, Mia cried her heart out that night. She tightly clutched onto my shoulders, not letting go.

"Mia," I said softly as I slowly patted her brown hair. "Stop joking... I would never leave you."

"That's what my parents told me... that's also what your parents told me when they adopted me... but they're all liars."

"Well, I'm not like them. I'm your brother. We'll be together forever and I'll never leave you." I talked real evenly, not startled by Mia at all.

"You promise?"

"Of course."

"You promise promise?" She asked again, this time holding out her pinky finger.

Seeing Mia doing this made me smirk. The last time we did a pinky promise together was probably around three years ago. I shrugged as I stuck out my pinky too, wrapping our two fingers together. " I pinky promise that I'd never leave you."

"Plus," I said again, "Why would I leave you anyways. You're the best little sister anyone could've possibly asked for. You're smart, understanding, you cook for me… and you're cute too!"

Despite her bawling from before, my words made the tips of Mia's mouth lift upwards into a grin. She said in a half-chuckle and half-teary voice, "Kai… why are you… like this…?"

"But seriously though. If it isn't because of your help, I wouldn't even be here right now. The only reason I'm able to leave you so freely is because you were able to take care of yourself, and you were even able to help me out."

"No…" Mia muttered. "You…"

"Do you deny it?" I asked, interrupting her. "You'd make food for me and clean up the entire house by yourself."

Mia was already slightly blushing now, she averted her gaze and pouted, "You're just trying to flatter me now."

"Mia…" I said as I slowly set her down so her foot touched the ground. "The truth is… I've always wanted to say this… thank you."

"Huh? What are you…?"

I knelt down slightly so I could be on the same eye level as her. Then I brushed off a few leftover teardrops on her face with my finger, as I said, "You're a big girl now. And big kids don't cry anymore."

"S-sorry."

"It's alright." I said, bringing Mia to me for a hug. "Let's go in the house"

Once we walked into the dining room, Mia took the curry rice she had already made, which had already gone cold, into the microwave to heat it up. I spent about an hour telling Mia about everything that happened at my school, even Ben and Ariya, as we ate. However, Mia surprisingly didn't make fun of me for pursuing Ariya, she was even quite impressed. "Congrats, Kai." She said when I finally wrapped up talking about my date with Ariya.

After finishing every single drop of rice and licking clean the sauce on my plate, I thanked Mia for making this delicious dinner and waved her goodnight. But before I could've went upstairs to my room, Mia said, "Kai? Can you come down to my room and sleep with me tonight?"

"Huh? Oh..." I muttered quietly.

"Please?" She pleaded, "It takes me so long to fall asleep myself... I'm scared."

"Aren't you a litte too old for that? How old are you?"

"You forgot how old I am?"

I laughed, making fun of her, "Just think about the stars in the heavens, that's what I do when I can't fall asleep."

"But..."

"I'm going to tell all your friends that you wanted your big brother to sleep with you."

"Please?" Mia begged again.

"Whatever, fine. Just because you were crying so hard earlier, I'll sleep with you just for one night."

"Yay!" Mia yelled in joy as she jumped up high into the air, "I'll be waiting for you in my room!"

I uncontrollably burst out into laughter as I ran up the stairs when I saw Mia's childish act. A moment earlier she was lecturing me about love, and now a second later she was too scared to sleep by herself.

"What's so funny?" Mia asked when she heard my giggles.

I stopped and yelled back in front of my door, "You are!"

It took me about fifteen minutes to shower and change into my navy blue pajamas. I gathered my pillow and blankets before going downstairs to Mia's room.

"Mia?" I asked as I knocked on her door, "Can I come in?"

"Yeah!" Mia yelled back.

I pushed the door open and walked in, even getting the chills when a gush of cold wind from the AC greeted me right in the face. "Where do you want me to sleep? On the floor?"

"No, of course not. You can sleep on the other side of the bed next to me."

I didn't even realize it before, but when I looked up at Mia after I set everything down, she was dressed in a light blue pajamas and had a teddy bear on her lap. Those two might not be significant objects, but they brought back a lot of memories between Mia and me - Her light blue pajamas was a matched pair to my navy blue ones we bought a year ago. Additionally, the teddy bear was my gift for Mia's seventh birthday, or her first birthday since joining my family.

"You still have Mika?" I said, pointing at the bear lying on her bed.

"You still remember her name?"

"Why would I forget it?" As I slipped under the covers, I turned to the left and said to Mia. "You named her with the first two letters of your name combined with the first two letters of my name."

With all the lights in her room turned off, the moonlight was able to make its way in through the undraped windows. "It's beautiful." I whispered.

"Yeah..." Mia nodded in agreement, smiling, "This feels really nostalgic...when was the last time we slept together?" Mia asked, laying her hand onto mine.

I thought about it for a while, but quietly muttered, "I don't know..."

Then Mia spoke up slowly. "I remember. It was four years ago. The night before the Meteors."

Even after she finished the sentence, the last word, Meteors, seemed to linger in the air for a while longer. That was the last time both of us said anything to each other for the rest of the night. Because when I turned around after a few minutes, Mia was already dreaming about the stars.

"*Jeez,*" I thought to myself, looking at the peaceful expression Mia had on her face, "*I thought it took you a while to fall asleep.*" Slowly shutting my eyes, I went to bed facing my little sister, with her hand in mine.

"Kai." Someone whispered next to me, it was a woman's voice.

"Yes? Mama?" I said as I lay on my bed, looking at the face directly above me. Her appearance was similar to mine. She had a short-bridged nose and a thin face. Her eyes were the same color as her dark, curly hair.

"You're going to get a little sister tomorrow." She whisperer into my ear.

"But your tummy isn't even round." Turning around, I pulled the blanket over my head, annoyed. "Where's she going to come from?" I groaned.

"It's different...she's going to come from somewhere else. But regardless, she's going to be your sister."

"All she's going to do is to steal you and dad's love away from me!" I shouted.

"Come on, Kai. You're already nine years old. Don't say that." My mom said as she took the blanket off my face. I tried to shield my eyes from her questioning gaze, but she was able to beat me to the punch. "She's going to be coming from a completely different family. Make sure to make her feel welcome because she will be living with us for her entire life now."

I quietly let out a sigh. It's not like I have much of a choice. "Whatever." I muttered.

"Weren't you always the one asking for a sibling so you'd have someone to play with?"

"But... that was just a spur of the moment thing... I didn't think you would actually get one."

"You should act like a big brother and take care of her." My mom said as she lowered her face, kissing me on the cheek. "Maybe you will become friends."

"Fine. I seriously doubt we will though."

"At least try to." My mom said as she got up from my bed and walked out of my room, turning off the light and shutting the door, "Alright, that's all. Good night, sweetie."

"Night."

"Hello, my name is Mia. Nice to meet you, everyone. Thank you for letting me stay with your family." The little girl said in a faint voice, with a trace of tears in her words. She had long, brown hair that flowed right to her shoulders. The girl was dressed in a pristine white skirt, her petite body reminded me of a field of virgin snow.

"Kai," My mom whispered into my ear, slowly nudging me forward, "Go introduce yourself."

I hesitated for a little bit. My head was wondering how will I ever get used to this person living under the same roof as me, when my mom nudged me again, still with a smile on her face. I started to walk toward her with short, but rapid steps. Even though the room we were in was only slightly over ten yards in length, it felt like it took me about an hour to get to the girl.

"Hey," I said, sticking out my hand, "I'm Kai. I guess I'm your big brother starting now."

"Big brother..." I repeated the words in my head. I didn't even realize the meaning of the words until now. I would have to take care of her everyday from now on. I would have to give her half of my toys and snacks. I thought, "why are my parents doing this anyway?"

However, the brown-haired girl standing in front, who was a head shorter than I was, reached out to me with both of her arms and took me into an embrace. "I always dreamed of having a big brother!" She yelled. " I hope we can get along with each other!"

I was utterly shocked by her reaction, and ashamed of myself. By the end of tonight, she would be sleeping in a completely different room, with a completely new environment, but she's even more optimistic than I am.

"Y-Yeah." I muttered slowly, at a loss of words. "I've always wanted a little sister too." I did not know why I said that, but those words simply rolled out of my mouth smoothly.

"Really?! This is so great!" Mia chirped loudly.

I suddenly heard my parents talking to the girl's counselor, who was a woman sitting behind a desk and held a few sheets of paperwork. "Kai was pretty negative about having her." My mom said as she took out a pen to sign a signature.

"Kai." The counselor said to my parents as she glanced at me, smiling. "He'll make a cool big brother. I know it."

For the first couple months after joining my family, I disliked Mia. She would enter my room without knocking, steal the TV remote from me and change the show to something she liked, and many other things. Sometimes she even asked me to play with her. She was a girl two years younger than me, how in the world would we share any common interests? Then one day, all my hate toward her suddenly evaporated into thin air, and flew away.

It was an early summer afternoon, three months after Mia's arrival. We were both on summer vacation already. Because I didn't have anything better to do, I agreed to play with her and to chase her around in our backyard.

Mia, dressed in a yellow T-shirt and some blue shorts, tripped over a piece of rock and fell, without warning. Because I wasn't able to stop myself, the two of us ended up colliding into each other and fell to the ground. "What are you doing?" I yelled.

"Kai..." She muttered.

"What?"

On contrary to my to hasty shouting, Mia's words were slow and soft, not startled at all. "I've had a lot of fun with you since coming here."

"Huh? Sarcasm?"

"No. I've had more fun in the three months here than I ever had since my parents died in a car accident when I was three." Mia explained.

The afternoon sun was beating down on us, making me sweat more just by being outside. Not understanding what Mia was trying to say, I got really agitated, "What're you saying?"

Instead of dropping the conversation, however, she continued, "Although you can be a little mean to me sometimes, you're still awesome to hang around with." She smiled.

"Oh... Thanks." I muttered, suddenly realizing how rude I was earlier.

"When I was back in the center with all the other homeless kids, we barely did anything for fun. I'm not going to explain the details because I don't want to think back, but my life here certainly is a lot better."

"Your life over at the center... was really that bad?" I've always simply assumed that the Adoption center offered the same things we did to Mia. So now when someone who actually lived in that place told me it was a lot worse, I was really surprised.

"Yeah, it was. We couldn't even leave the building. They'd only give us a tiny amount of food. Everything wasn't enough. Not enough happiness, not enough friends, not enough space, and not enjoying enough of life." Mia said quietly, her eyes staring at the grass on the ground. "Living here with your family has taught me that."

I didn't know why, but perhaps it was because it was my first time thinking about what Mia actually went through at such a young age, I somehow found myself sympathizing with her. I said without even realizing it, " Yeah... don't worry about it. I'm always here... for you."

I could see Mia's eyes getting wet, she sniffles, "T-thanks, Kai."

"And... it's not my family, it's our family."

It was the first time someone called me that. My heart shook, and the barrier between Mia and me crumpled away.

5

Unlike any other day when I woke up at the crack of dawn, today was the first time I slept in all the way until ten o'clock. When I woke up, my face felt a little different than before. My hand quickly flew up to check what was wrong, finally realizing that my cheeks were damp with tears. At first I was a little confused, then I remembered the dream I had about Mia's past. "Huh?" I murmured out loud, quickly turning my head to my left. Only to find Mia staring right into my eyes.

"Kai! What are you doing?" Mia gasped as she kicked me in the legs.

"Ow!" I screeched in pain. "What was that?"

Mia muttered, as if she had done nothing wrong, "Why did you turn around so quickly, only to stare at me?!"

"You were staring at me in the first place." I said, walking out of the room. "Well, I'm in a good mood today, I'm not going to argue with you so early in the morning."

As I closed the door to Mia's room behind me, I could still hear Mia rolling around and making weird noises at me.

Because Ariya was doing a physical exam and Ben was still minding his own business, I didn't know what to do today.

I went out and bought some groceries in the morning and stayed in my room for the rest of the day. Occasionally, when I came downstairs to get water or some snacks, I'd bump into Mia, who would be doing the same thing.

As hours and hours passed by, I laid in bed at night and muttered to myself, "Today might not be the most interesting day, but I got a lot of homework done and packed everything for the school trip." I couldn't believe that the trip was only three day away!

The next day was Monday, and I prepared myself for another boring day of school. I woke up relatively early, did my regulars, grabbed breakfast, which Mia has already made the night before, and went to school quickly. The weather wasn't perfect. Instead of a completely clear sky from yesterday and the day before, there were a few clouds dancing around.

Just when I thought today was going to be boring like always, I saw a blond girl sitting in a wheelchair, surrounded by classmates as I walked into the classroom. "Ariya! I yelled, rushing over to her desk, "You're here today? How did it heal so quickly?"

She was wearing the white shirt of her school uniform, but had her own pants on. Ariya managed to mouth me a *"I'll talk to you later"* as she got bombarded with questions from other classmates such as *"Oh my god! What happened to you?"*

Ben walked into the classroom a few minutes later. However, he didn't even seem fazed when he saw Ariya in her wheelchair. "Hey." He said, waving at her casually.

At first, I didn't know why Ben was acting so calm; but then I realized Ariya must've told him she was coming to school beforehand. Knowing that she talked to Ben before telling me caused my body to stir.

"Alright!" Mr. Eric said as he made his way to the front of the room. "As you can see, Ariya is attending school with her injuries, but she needs someone to help her get around. So… which one of you will be kind enough to lend her a helping hand?"

Over half of the classmates raised their hands without hesitation, which included all of the boys, even Ben, but I was the only exception. "Who wouldn't want to make a good impression on Ariya?" Someone said quietly from the back of the room.

"Well?" Mr. Eric gestured to Ariya, "Your pick."

She glanced slowly around the room, as if looking for someone. I thought she was searching for Ben, but her gaze soon blew past him and ended up locking onto mine. She smiled and said out loud, "Why not the only boy who didn't raise his hand? Kai?"

Ariya's words caused a few murmurs to stir in the room. I could already hear some people gossiping about me. "Uh…" I muttered, looking at Ariya with an unsure expression, "Are you sure?"

"Awww, come on." Ariya pleaded. "It's just for helping me around. You won't regret it."

I threw my hands up in the air as if giving up, and said resignedly,but my inside was drowning in happiness, " Fine. I'll do it."

As Ariya shot me a thumbs up and laughed, I couldn't help but to steal a glance at Ben with the edge of my vision. But instead of finding his usual easygoing smile, I saw a clouded and confused gaze.

The first period of the day soon ended. The first thing I did after the bell rang was to hurry over to Ariya's desk, "How are you at school already? I thought you needed at least a few more days."

"Nah," Ariya answered, stuffing her books into her backpack, "my exam yesterday was a success. Everything else beside my legs had already been taken care of."

I felt a few gazes looking at us, but I didn't pay attention to any of them. Because right now, as far as I'm concerned, nothing matters to me except for Ariya. I smiled as I patted her gently on the shoulder, "That's really good to hear! Congrats!"

"So I can probably go on the school trip in a couple of days too." Ariya added.

"Fantastic!"

By the time Ariya and I were done talking, we were already the last two people in the room. The bell of next class was already about to ring as well.

"Ready to leave?" I asked.

Ariya nodded in response. "We have next period together, right?"

"Yup." I said as I pushed her wheelchair out of the room and into the hallway. Our next class was English, which was on the second floor of the building. Because Ariya had her wheelchair and couldn't use the stairs, we had to use to the elevator on the other side of the building to get upstairs.

We finally made it into the room after a little bit, but class had already begun three minutes ago. Additionally, everyone was staring at Ariya and me when we entered, making the situation even more awkward. And it wasn't until after helping Ariya to her seat that I realized I had left my own backpack downstairs in homeroom. "Excuse me." I said quietly to the teacher, "Can I go get my backpack from downstairs?"

The English teacher didn't seem too impressed with me, but she nodded anyways because she knew I had to help Ariya out.

I sprinted out of the room and ran down the stairs, skipping two at a time. As expected, my backpack was under my seat when I darted in to homeroom. But just as I grabbed it quickly and was about to hurry back up, I heard a beeping sound over the school speakers and then the alarm went off at a deafening volume.

"Attention everyone! This is not a drill! There is an uninvited visitor on campus, possibly carrying a weapon. The school will now go into lockdown. Please proceed to the nearest shelter and follow the teachers' instructions."

"What on earth?" I gasped, "Are you serious?" This was something I had only seen in movies before. An actual criminal was on campus, and we weren't even a week into school yet.

Looking across the hall, many of the students in the other classrooms were already evacuating and running. Some were shouting, "Where's the shelter room?!" To make everything easier, the teachers told us to proceed to the gymnasium as fast as possible so it would be easier to look after us if we were all in one place.

With all of the students rushing out of the rooms all at once in an attempt to reach the gym, which was located in another building, the entire hallway was cramped and barely moving. To make matters worse, everyone was shouting at each other and nobody could hear the instructions over all the noise. Of course, realizing that there might be a chance of actually dying here, it wasn't a surprise that our instincts of survival kicked in and began to escape, throwing away all manners aside. It took me about three minutes to get to the door at the end of the hallway and out of the current academic building. Once I did, I breathed in a huge gulp of fresh air and continued to the sports arena.

"The intruder is currently on the other side of the campus!" A security guard yelled as we entered the gym and lined up by grade levels. Normally, everyone would be chatting with their peers right now, but perhaps it was the tight space or perhaps it was the nervous atmosphere, nobody said a single word to each other. With the only exception of a few people who were praying for their safety.

"Has everyone left the two academic buildings and the science center?" The headmaster asked.

"Junior class is all here!" A teacher yelled.

"Same for the seniors!"

"Sophomore class is all set as well!"

Listening to those pleasant reports, I thought we were extremely lucky to have everyone successfully evacuated. However, when I turned around to look at Me. Eric, who was still counting our numbers, I noticed the hopelessness on his face.

"I counted multiple times, but freshman class is missing one." He said at last.

Everyone gasped at Mr. Eric's words. A few were already in tears. "Do you know who?" The headmaster of the school asked from the front of the gym.

"I don't have my attendance sheet with me." Me. Eric said, shaking his head.

I was also trying to figure out who that unlucky person was. However, when I did, my heart sank to the rock bottom. I didn't even want to believe it was the truth at first, but once I scanned the faces of my classmates, it was painfully clear.

"Ariya!" I shouted, shattering the silence in the room, "Ariya's missing." I couldn't help what I did next, but I sprinted out of the line and out of the exit. Many of the teachers were yelling at me to come back, but there was no way I was going to without Ariya.

Surprisingly, the campus was dead quiet as I stepped outside. Instead of the constant shouting and laughing of students I would normally hear in school, the only thing audible to the ear right now is my heavy breathing and the brushing sound of the light wind.

Knowing the intruder could be coming at me at any second, or possibly even with a gun, I concentrated on hiding myself instead of running as fast as I could. I knew Ariya couldn't move quickly without someone's help, so I concluded she must still be in the academic building, and that's where I was going.

The walk that normally would've taken me only three minutes ended up taking about ten, as I was constantly paying close attention to my surroundings. I'd snap around even if it's just the rustling of a single leaf or the squeak of a bird. Thankfully, I was able to make it to the building without any trouble.

Just as I was about to enter the academic building, I realized the door wouldn't open. "*What did I expect? This thing is called a lockdown. So of course everything is going to be locked.*" I tried charging at the wooden door and knocking it down like I did in Ariya's hospital room, but this was almost five times the size of a regular door and weighed more than a huge stone boulder.

I suddenly heard the noises of glass shattering coming from the other side of the building as I paced around the obstacle blocking my way. My body froze in fear; my arms and legs shook uncontrollably. It was at that moment I realized how dangerous of a situation I was in. I was literally risking my life trying to save someone who I was not even sure liked me back. "*Is this really worth it?*" I asked myself.

I chuckled, "Who am I kidding?" Saying the words out loud, as I answered my own question, "What will be left of my life if Ariya is gone?" I picked up a huge rock lying next to a plant and hurled it as hard as I could toward the glass window to the left of the huge wooden door. Luckily, the impact shattered the glass and the entire window came flying off.

Immediately after, I dove inside the building and hid myself under a desk, praying to God that the intruder didn't know my precise location. After catching my breath, I noticed the messy state the classrooms were in. All of the lights were shut off. Many of the chairs and tables were knocked over. And there were trash lying all over the place as well. I waited patiently for a minute and made sure there was no movements near me. Then, I made a run for the stairs and arrived at the second floor, the floor Ariya was on. *"Ariya… please be safe! Please let me get to her before any bad things happen to her!"*

I dashed to the English classroom as fast as possible which was located at the end of the hallway. However, as I got half way through the corridor, I heard heavy footsteps coming from the same stairs I was just walking on a minute ago. "Damn it!" I cursed under my breath, "Why do you have to come now!?"

"Ariya." I said as I knocked on the door to the English room, controlling my volume so it was loud enough for someone inside the room to hear, but quiet enough so the intruder who was in the stairwell at the other end of the hallway wouldn't.

Silence

I unfolded the curtain blocking the small window on the door. When I peeked inside, I found a pitch dark room with all of the shades drawn. I simply stood there, in front of the door, too shocked to believe my eyes. "Where is she?" I asked as I looked back inside and searched the place for one more time, not giving up just yet. Suddenly, I saw something in the far corner of the dark room, toppled over. It was Ariya's wheelchair, with someone leaning against it on the ground. Her messy blond hair obscured her face from my view. She sat there silently, staring at the ground, drowning in despair.

"Ariya!" I knocked on the door again, more rapidly this time as the sound of footsteps drew closer and louder by the second. "I'm Kai! Open the door!"

Unlike last time, my voice was able to reach her. Ariya's head spun up and searched desperately for the speaker as soon as she heard it. When she saw me at last, Ariya crawled over to the door with her two hands and pulled me into the room, just before the intruder was able to step foot onto this floor.

On contrary to the desperate look she had before, her eyes were already sparkling with tears soon after seeing me. "I thought…" Ariya said as she hugged me tightly, "I thought you guys were just going to leave me…"

"Don't you worry about that, Ariya. We'd never leave you behind. I'd never leave you behind." I assured her, tightly embracing her body.

"Thanks."

I pointed at the closet on the other side of the room, "Someone is still outside. Let's get in there so he wouldn't see us."

After lowering my body so Ariya could get onto my back, I darted to the other side of the room and hid ourselves into the piece of furniture, which barely had enough space to fit the two of us. It wasn't long after that, when I heard a gunshot, followed by footsteps entering our room.

"Get behind me." I quietly whispered to Ariya inside the tiny cubicle, barely able to maintain myself from cracking under the immense pressure. Even if one of us two made a peep of sound loud enough for the man outside to hear, it wouldn't matter how heroic I was, we would be dead for sure.

Without hesitation or doubt, Ariya listened to me and did what I told her. After she quietly scooched her body to the space behind me, I fully extended my arms upwards, planning to block the first few gunshots for her if the man decided to check the closet.

Ariya, perhaps sensing my intentions, wrapped her arms around me and sobbed silently, her tears dripping onto my shoulder. Through the tiny crack of the two doors of the closet, I was able to see the person. He was a tall man wearing clothes of full black and a creepy clown mask, holding a rifle in his right hand.

The gunman paced around the room for a while, as if searching for something. Then without warning, he stopped right in front of the closet Ariya and I were hiding in. My heart was pounding. It was beating so intensely I thought it was going to jump out of my throat. I glanced nervously at Ariya, whose face was resting on my shoulder, to check how she was holding up. Through the painful look she had on her face and how tightly her arms were wrapped around my body, I could tell she was on the brink of collapsing as well.

Through the tiny aperture of the doors, I saw the man in black reach out for the closet handle. If he pulled on it now, there would be nothing we could do. However, that's when I heard the sirens of the police cars pulling up the street, followed by a loud explosion somewhere in the same building.

"*Tsk.*" Realizing the cops were now here, the intruder groaned as he gave the closet a wicked kick in frustration, then scurried his way out of the room.

The moment I heard the sound of the sirens and the voices of the policemen, I sighed in relief and thought the nightmare would be over soon and the man would retreat immediately. As a result, I was totally taken off guard when he drew back his leg and punted the doors right in front of me. The force of the kick caused the wooden structure to smash directly into my face, and knocking me out of consciousness. Ariya was able to catch me as I was falling backwards. "Kai!" She yelled after making sure the intruder was gone. "Kai! Wake up! Wake up!"

When I opened my eyes again, the first thing I saw was an unfamiliar white ceiling. I tried turning my head, but then noticed something was tightly wrapped around it. "What is… this?" I murmured quietly as I sat up on the bed. Now that I was able to see the entire room, I realized I was in a hospital. There was another person in the room. Ironically enough, she wore the same white shirt I had on, which showed she was also a patient here. However, it looked like she was the one taking care of me when I slept.

"You're finally awake." The girl said, rolling her wheelchair closer to my bed. "That took a while."

"Oh, Ariya. I couldn't have slept for too long, right?" Looking out of the window in my room, I saw pitch darkness with a few sparkling stars hanging in the sky. "So I fell asleep.... This afternoon? It has only been a few hours." As I tried to recall what happened with the school lockdown, every drop of my memory came flooding back into my head.

Ariya shook her head, "You were out for one whole day and a few hours."

"What?! Seriously?"

Ariya nodded silently in response, then pointed at something lying on top of the nightstand next to a lamp. It was a bouquet of beautiful flowers, with a mix of the orange Chrysanthemums, white Lilies, and red Roses.

"Wow... " I muttered as I took it, the intoxicating scent rushing into my nose "Who brought it?"

"It was a gift from everybody. All your friends contributed."

"That's nice..." I muttered, " What did the school do about the lockdown? Did anyone get hurt?"

"No one was injured besides you." Ariya explained, "Some parts of the buildings were severely damaged. School will be canceled for the next two weeks. On top of that, because the headmaster of the school didn't want to simply give us two weeks of free vacation, they're giving us one extra day for the orientation trip, we're going to leave today instead of tomorrow, and we'll stay there for two nights. In a few hours, we'll meet in front of the school."

"That's not too bad." I muttered, "It honestly could've gone a lot worse."

"Yeah." Ariya nodded, "Are you still going on the trip?"

"Of course! Why wouldn't I? I already packed everything a few days ago."

Ariya pointed at the bandage around me head, "But your injuries..."

"I'm fine." I said, taking the white bandage off my head and wrapped it around my hand, "See? There was barely anything to begin with. It already healed anyway."

Ariya pointed at the trash can at the corner of the room, "You can throw it out there."

"Nah." I replied as I fumbled the bandage around my hand.

"You're gonna keep it?" Ariya asked, raising an eyebrow, "Why?"

Thinking back to the lockdown, I couldn't even remember what my motivation was for blocking the danger for Ariya. As I sat on the hospital bed and clutching the bandage in my right hand, I answered, "It's the proof, the symbol for me sacrificing myself to save you."

"Yeah," Ariya started, "I didn't even get the chance to say it yet, but I want to thank you.. I was stuck by myself in that room…I felt so hopeless and thought it was only a matter of time before the man finds me… I thought I would've died for sure. But when I saw you at the door, I thought you were an angel for a second… I was so relieved!"

Just thinking about the memories of that incident was terrifying enough for Ariya to shed tears. I walked to her wheelchair and knelt down, bringing her body close to my mine. "It's all in the past now. You're here, safe with me." I whispered into her ear.

"I don't regret choosing you as my helper that morning." Ariya said suddenly, in the middle of her tears.

All the trouble and the pain I went through, in the end my reward was a simple line of thanks. But for me, that was already enough. "Hearing these words of appreciation from you… I don't regret choosing to help you either."

When I glanced down at Ariya's face, patting her back, I saw something I've been searching for. She looked at me with a pair of earnest eyes, her tips of her lips sprung upwards in an arc. Even though the last time I saw this expression of her's was four years ago, it wasn't something I would ever forget. "No, you're the angel." I said slowly, our gazes meeting, "Ariya, you're beautiful."

6

Mia's initial reaction to me leaving for the school trip was reluctance and sadness. She ran up to me on the front porch of my house and wouldn't let go of my arm. I thought it was really sweet that Mia cared about me so much and didn't want me to leave her, but knowing that she couldn't rely on me forever, she eventually let go.

"Mia." Turning around, I said to her as I was about to leave, "You're always been the one taking care of the house and even me. You've been doing this for the entire time, you just haven't realized it yet."

"I don't know if I can handle the entire house by myself though, especially at night." Mia complained, "I'll also get lonely."

I dropped my suitcase and backpack onto the ground, then slowly walked over to my little sister for a farewell embrace. "It's only for two nights. I believe in you" I whispered into Mia ears.

As I picked up my belongings and continued down the street, sometimes turning around to check on Mia. She stood in front of our house, one hand was holding onto a handkerchief while her other hand was waving at me the entire time, With a final turn when I reached the end of the street, her small figure disappeared from my view.

Dressed in the plainest clothing possible, I arrived at school and saw the group of my classmates gathered around the entrance with all of their bags, already loading onto the school bus for our trip. "Yo Kai!" Ben yelled as soon as he saw me, he was wearing his yellow soccer jersey again because there weren't any dress code requirement,"Nice job on saving Ariya back there! I honestly I didn't think you were going to make it back alive when you ran out of the gym." Many other classmates high-fived and fist-bumped me as well.

"I didn't think I was going to survive either." I said as I stowed my suitcase into the storage area under the bus. "But I guess I got lucky."

After our reunion introduction was finished, our grade, sixty students, filed onto the bus, two people per row of seats. I wanted to sit next to Ariya, but the teachers said she had to sit by herself in the front of the bus because of her wheelchair. Luckily, Ben was by himself when I got on, so I plopped myself down next to him. We waited for another minute or two for everyone to get on, then we were on our way to the camp.

At first, I thought the bus ride was going extremely boring because we weren't allowed to bring our phones with us on the trip. However, it turned out to be not boring at all. Every once in a while, a few classmates would ask me about what happened when I was rescuing Ariya in the lockdown. There were even a few rumors about us doing other things as we were in the room together. Ben, however, didn't seem that interested in what we were talking about. He leaned his head against the window, quietly minding his own business.

Besides chatting with my classmates and friends, the view outside the vehicle was gorgeous and entertaining too. As we left the city and pulled onto the highway, the number of buildings and structures surrounding the road decreased dramatically as well. The stillness of the cloudless, azure sky extending infinitely past the horizon greatly contradicted the busy, city life we just experienced not long ago. Additionally, the sunshine would sometimes make its way into the bus, casting a warm layer of light onto my skin.

I would occasionally steal a few glances at Ariya, who was sitting in the first row. Every time I did so, she would either be staring outside the window aimlessly or sitting with her eyes closed. A few classmates tried asking her about what happened in her perspective of the lockdown, but the near-death experience must've really shaken her up, making her wave their questions off.

While I was talking to my other classmates and enjoying the scenery, the three hour bus ride felt like it passed by in the blink of an eye. The camp itself was located in the middle of an enormous forest. Many wooden cabins scattered across the wide campus entered my view as we drove in. There were a lot of different reactions from classmates when they saw them. Some didn't like the rural features and the simplicity of them, while others loved their natural impression. The driver finally parked the car in a clearing amidst the thick trees, next to a big, white tent about the size of a with signs saying "Camp Mirage Center".

Although the drive wasn't that long and we were still in the same district of land, this place covered by greens felt completely alien to the city I lived in. "Ahhh! Fresh air!" Some of the kids chirped as we got off the bus and unloaded our luggage.

After settling down, the chaperones gathered us in the main tent, which had rows of wooden tables and long benches, and announced the camp rules. Because I had to help Ariya get off the bus, the two of us joined the rest of the group a few minutes later. The two of the most important rules were that everyone had curfew of ten o'clock at night, in addition with boys and girls weren't allowed to visit each other's cabins. Afterwards, lunch was served to us in the same center building. There were two options for the meal, either burgers or curry rice. I went with the latter option. I quickly got my food tray from the counter, and walked to the table Ariya and Ben were sitting at. I wasn't too excited to find those two together again, excluding me, despite how I saved her. I tried to shake that annoyance away, and put up a smile on my face instead.

"Hey, Kai!" Ariya waved at me as soon as I sat down. She was wearing the grey T-shirt we bought together with the little white kitten sewn at the front.

"What's up?" I said, parking myself in the spot next to Ben.
"How are you liking the camp so far?" She asked.

As I scanned the inside of the big, windowless tent we were in, besides the rows of tables and benches, there was a huge fireplace positioned right in front of the center of the back wall. Furthermore, instead of using regular light bulbs and electricity as the lightings, the entire place illuminated by candlelights. "I don't know about you, but I think it's nice for us to go to a place for a change." I replied at last.

Ariya nodded, "Especially if you've been stuck in a hospital room for almost room for almost a week."

"Come on, guys. Let's not forget to eat. I'm starving!" Ben said as he bit into his burger, "It's so good!" He exclaimed with a mouthful of food.

"Yeah! It is really good!" Ariya agreed, chewing on hers as well. "Kai, why did you get the rice option?"

"I don't know... " I muttered, poking the pieces chicken on my plate with a fork, "I guess I've had a lot of western food recently and wanted a break."

Taking another bite from the burger, Ariya smiled happily, "You're certainly missing out on a lot of good stuff here."

"Whatever, there's going to be more meals here."

After finishing up the food and clearing the plates, our class gathered together and received our room assignments. It was four students per cabin, and the teacher picked out our roommates based on who we usually hung out with at school.

The name of my cabin was called the "Red Birds". I wasn't surprised to find out that Ben rooming as me, but I was feeling both positive and negative toward it. I was happy that at least one of my only friends were with me, but somehow I also thought I've had enough of him for a while.

One of the other two classmates was another friend of Ben's. On contrary to Ben's tall and slender build, his friend, Andrew, was a chubby, friend fellow who I sometimes talked to at school. He had short, spiky, black hair and would sometimes yell a random joke and make our entire class laugh. Lastly, his slightly-darker-than-average skin color revealed his different origin than the rest of us.

Lastly, the final person that was going to share the same cabin as us, Kevin, was an unlucky outsider. According to him, he just recently moved to the city and everything was new to him. He didn't talk to anyone at school, nor did he have any friends. He wore glasses, and had long, light blond hair that reached his shoulders.

As the four of us received our room key and slowly strolled to our cabin together in the woods, we spotted many wild animals such as deer, rabbits, or raccoons dashing and running all over the place. It took us a few minutes to find our cabin. When we did, it was in the middle of the forest and completely surrounded by thick trees, which were the size of five-story buildings, some already turning half orange because of the season. We couldn't even hear the noises and shouts of the other students because the cabins were so distant from each other. It was like we were isolated from the rest of the class, in a world of our own.

There were two rooms inside the cabin, each consisted of two twin beds and a table. There was barely enough room for the four of us, but it wasn't crowded either.

"Hey!" Andrew shouted as he leapt straight across the first room and landed on the bed with the biggest window, "I'm sleeping on this one!"

I didn't really care who would be my roommate or which bed I would sleep in because they looked all the same to me. Walking pass the bathroom, I opened the door and entered the second room. To my surprise, after I plopped myself down onto one of the two open beds, Ben followed me in a minute later and took the other one.

Peering through the small window next to my bed, I couldn't believe what my eyes eyes seeing. "Oh my!" I exclaimed as I darted out of the room through the backdoor. The other three soon followed me out as well.

A river with a few yards in width lay right in front of our eyes. As I ran across the grassy field all the way to its edge and stuck my hand into the water, I was stunned by its clarity and how cold it was even though the sun was shining on us directly overhead. It was by no means a big or impressive stream; in fact, it was barely a foot deep. There were little stone pebbles lying on its bottom, with a few bigger ones peaking their tops over the water, scattered sporadically. I tried to follow the river with my eyes and see where the water originated from or where it was headed to, but it soon extended out of my view on both ends. Along with the other creatures and fishes that called the river home, despite its slow speed, it was alive and flowing.

The four of us stood on the bank, still admiring its beauty. It was as if the river emanated a special charm of silence, because rather than talking to each other and joking, all we could hear right now was the light chirping of birds and the soft gushing of the creek.

After about another fifteen minutes or so, we finally returned to our cabin. On our way back, I noticed the outside of the river was completely surrounded by trees and bushes, fully hiding its existence. The only place someone could see it was through the same opening near our cabin.

One of the things the chaperones said during our lunch meeting was that there were multiple activities, such as football or archery, happening simultaneously at different locations on campus. We had the option to either attend those or to do whatever we wanted as long as we stayed within the vicinity of the camp. I didn't know what I should do for the rest of the afternoon, so I decided to go back to the camp center and check out the activities catalogue.

Just as I ambled on the main road of the camp by myself, I saw two girls behind me, coming from their side of the camp. One of them was Ariya, the other one was pushing her wheelchair. "Oh Kai!" Ariya waved as she saw me, "Can you take over for her? She's already out of breath here."

"Come on! Give me a break!" The other girl yelled behind Ariya's wheelchair. Her name was Jenny. She was relatively tall, and had a bowl cut with her deep black hair. "I'm pushing you uphill!"

"Sure," I turned around and walked back toward them.

Jenny passed the wheelchair handles to me as soon as I got there, then took off running into the distance, "Thank! Bye!"

"Wow…" I muttered awkwardly, slowly pushing her wheelchair, "That was quick."

Shaking her head, Ariya said quietly, "Almost nobody in my cabin wanted to help me get around. Jenny was the only one who even agreed to push me to the center."

"Well, not everyone's perfect."

Ariya nodded in agreement, but stayed quiet for the rest of the way. We were moving slightly slower than walking speed because the dirt road in the camp was very bumpy and unstable. The afternoon sun would sometimes peek its head over the thick trees and leaves overhead. Despite the sunshine once in a while, the shades caused by the trees and the fresh scent of autumn leaves brought a few chills in the air.

After a few minutes of walking, we arrived at the big bulletin board near the center tent. A printed schedule of today's activities was pinned onto it. The options were basketball. football, soccer, volleyball, archery, and mini golf. "Anything interests you?" I said to Ariya after finishing reading the entire list.

"I don't know… It's not like I can participate in any." Ariya murmured. "Do you have any ideas?"

"Uh… Well… The thing is, I don't play any of these sports. So I really can't choose…"

"In that case," Ariya said at last, "Let's go to the soccer field. I bet Ben's there kicking the ball around. We can go watch him play."

Instantly after hearing Ariya's remark, the first word that popped into my head was "no". Seeing how Ariya and Ben acted together during lunch was already enough to make me nauseous, I certainly wasn't looking forward to spending an entire afternoon with them. "Are you sure?" I asked, wishing that Ariya would change her mind.

Unable to read the expression on my face, however, Ariya pointed her hand toward the direction of the soccer field to the right and shouted with a grin on her face, "Yeah! You two can even play each other!"

Obviously, Ben, being the captain of the soccer team, was better than me at the sport. So the last thing I needed was to have him completely obliterate me in front of Ariya. But, of course, there was no way I was going to say that to her, so I ended up listening to Ariya and began pushing her wheelchair to the right.

"Hey!' Ben, dressed in his flashy jersey, yelled at Ariya and me from the soccer field a mile away as he scored goals after goals on some classmates. The edge of his eyes were probably constantly checking the field's entrance, praying for Ariya to come watch him showoff.

Ariya signaled me to hurry up. Once I pushed we cleared the muddy road and got onto the grass, I parked her wheelchair onto the side, under the shade of the enormous trees surrounding the field. Ariya cheered loudly once we got closer, "Nice goal!"

Standing behind Ariya, I thought it would be rude of me to not say anything, so I waved at him as well, "Hey Ben."

I expected him to get annoyed when he saw me with Ariya again, because I imagined he would want some private time with her once in a while. But on the contrary to what I thought, instead of getting mad, Ben casually gestured me to play with him and the other classmates.

I shook my head at first, still didn't want Ben to humiliate me. But Ariya soon turned around and nudged me as well. Eventually, my wall of defense fell apart when Ben said he wanted me to join his team so we could play two people versus two people using one net. "Come on." He said again.

"It's just a game of soccer, how bad can it be?" I muttered to myself as I slowly walked onto the field and joined the Ben with the other two.

As the mini-sized game started, anyone would've been able to tell that I was a newbie. I charged at the ball aimlessly despite getting juked left and right. Sure, Ben was a skilled player, but I didn't think he would be able to do anything against two opponents when I was such a burden.

He tried passing the ball to me multiple times, but I ended up missing all of the shots, either sending it flying or getting blocked. I could even hear Ariya cracking up at my misses on the side. Whenever we took a break and I left the grassfield to get water from the side, Ariya would pat me on the back and tell me I did pretty good out there, which I knew was a blatant lie.

One time on the field, Ben single-handedly blew past the two opponents. But instead of scoring an open goal, he decided to give me another chance and passed the ball to me. For any other soccer player, it would've been an easy goal, being so close to the net. But it felt like miles away for me. Knowing I had a limited amount of time before the defenders were able to recover, I took a small step to the left and punted the ball as hard as possible with my eyes closed, too scared to see the result.

I thought I would hear Ben's sympathetic words again on how I shouldn't give up yet and how the next shot would be better. But to my pleasant surprise, I heard Ariya's loud cheering and Ben practically jumped on top of me in celebration. "There you go, Kai!"

As I slowly opened my eyes, a beam of sunlight escaped the cover of the clouds and shone brightly on us, blinding me. When I blocked the glare with my hand, I saw the black-and-white soccer ball lying still in the net. "Wow, I finally did it." I said at last.

"Yup! You did!" Walking over to me and patting me on the shoulders, Ben said, "I never doubted you, buddy."

Glancing at Ben and Ariya on the side, who was still clapping and cheering me on, I thought to myself, *"Ben, stop being so nice to me. You're the bad guy here. You're the one taking Ariya away from me. But you're making it hard for me to hate you…"*

We played soccer for another hour or two after that, all the way until the sun was just beginning to descend down the trees and out of our view. As we said goodbye to our two classmates who played with us, Ben, Ariya, and I slowly ambled back toward the main tent for dinner. I was pushing Ariya in her wheelchair, while Ben walked next to me. His hand suddenly flew to his pocket and his said quietly, "Hey guys, can you wait up? Let's take a picture together."

"With what?" I asked.

Ben searched our surroundings carefully, making sure nobody else was present.Then he said as he took out his phone, "With this!"

"What?" Ariya chimed in, "But you weren't allowed to bring it."

"Don't worry. I'm fine if nobody else sees it."

"Is risking getting your phone taken away worth it for one picture?" I said, "I mean, we can get the picture anytime, it doesn't have to be on this trip."

Ben hesitated, his head was staring at the dirt under his shoes. "It's nice to have all these trees as our background." He finally replied, "Anyway, selfie time! Say cheese!"

Ben stood slightly in front of me and ariya, raising his phone high above his head. We stared straight into the camera and made a few funny faces. Then, with a "click!" sound, that picture of us three was recorded permanently into his phone. "Nice!" He commented as he opened his album, "Thanks, guys."

Dinner was average, definitely wasn't as great as today's lunch. Instead of getting to pick what we eat, the only option was spaghetti with meatballs, and it wasn't even that good. Ariya, Ben, and I sat together at a table with some other classmates like always. We talked about sports, music, and games, pretty much what someone would expect at a dinner table with high-schoolers. The temperature dropped significantly compared to the afternoon, when we'd sweat by wearing only shorts and T-shirts. The few gushes of cold air that escaped inside when someone occasionally opened the tent flap was enough to give us the chills.

Looking at the schedule, there wasn't anything planned after dinner, so we headed back to our cabins after we ate. Before sending us to bed, however, the chaperones gathered us at a common area next to a fire pit in the open and went through some rules for the night, with the most important one being that we weren't allowed to leave our cabin until daybreak.

After the meeting was finished, I pushed Ariya back to her cabin on the other side of the campus, which took about ten minutes. By the time I got to the girls' side of camp, the sun had already completely set. There weren't any street lamps, as a result, everywhere I went was almost pitch black. With this being our first day here, I still wasn't one hundred percent sure on where to go. I had to rely on the measly amounts of light emitted from the other cabins scattered sporadically around the main road to read the signs and see the walkway ahead. Every so often, I'd hear some weird noises coming from the bushes surrounding me, but I simply hustled up my footsteps and tried my best to not pay any attention to them. In the end, after twenty minutes of getting lost and hitting my head by stumbling into trees, I was finally standing in front of the door to my cabin.

"Kai!" Ben, dressed in his grey nightgowns already, yelled as he opened the wooden door, letting me in. "Where were you this entire time?"

"I was helping Ariya," I muttered, too tired to explain anything, "But got lost on my way back."

Andrew sat up from his bed and chimed into the conversation as well, "At least tell us something when you leave. We thought you were snatched off by a bear or something."

"I know, I know... " I answered lazily, making a beeline for my bed in the other room. "How do you guys still have energy left? I'm exhausted!"

Ben walked into our room and climbed into his bed, "Who told you we weren't tired? We were just talking about how worn out we were before you came in."

"That's enough talking for now, Kai still needs to shower and change." Kevin, who has been lying in his bed the entire time, suddenly spoke up, "We can chat in bed when he's done."

I wasn't too happy with the commanding tone Kevin had, but like I said before, my body was too fatigued to do the arguing. "Fine." I grunted loudly as I walked over into the bathroom between the two rooms.

When I got out of the shower, changed into my navy blue pajamas, and opened the bathroom door, the two oil lamps in each of the two bedrooms had already been extinguished. Fortunately, with the help of the moonlight through the windows, I was able to make my way back to my bed without tripping over any of the bags lying on the floor.

"So much for chatting after I shower. They're already dead asleep." I muttered to myself as I lay in bed, listening to them snoring away.

Turning my head away from the room, I stared out the window in the wall. Before, when I was in the city, I could barely see the moon behind the cloudy night, let alone the tiny stars. But right now, when we were sleeping in the elements, there wasn't a single cloud nor obstacle blocking the view. I gazed at this nature's harmony in yearning, losing myself in its beauty. This scene, the shining glow of the moon accompanied with the countless amounts of stars sparkling in the sky was so alluring and peaceful, I forever etched it into my heart.

I forgot how easy it was to lose track of time when I was doing something I enjoyed. By the time I spun around and looked back inside the room, it was already almost midnight. However, a voice spoke up abruptly and almost gave me a heart attack. It was Ben's. "Can't fall asleep?" He asked.

"No, the view is too pretty. I can't help but to look outside." I said softly, careful not to wake up the two classmates in the other room.

From where I was sleeping, I saw Ben staring out his window as well. He had a smile on his face, but it was as still as a statue, "Me neither." He whispered.

"I've never seen you so quiet before. You've always been the energetic type."

Ben responded, "Well, it's my first time seeing your peaceful and artistic side too."

"Really?" I said. I wasn't able to see his face in the darkness, but I knew he was also looking back at me. "We've known each other for so long, but there are still so many things we don't know."

"Yeah…"

"We have to hangout more." I suggested, "We can go to the movies, amusement parks, or even another arcade. It'll be fun."

Silence…

It was a minute later when Ben made another sound, "Thanks, Kai." He said faintly.

"For what?"

I never heard him answer my question. Because the next time I turned my head to look at him, he was already sound asleep.

Before I knew it, the sun was already up and so was Kevin and Andrew in the other room. With all of the ruckus they were making when they brushed their teeth and got changed, it was practically impossible for Ben and me to sleep. "What time is it?" I muttered as I opened my eyes and stared at the dark wooden ceiling hazily. When I finally came to my consciousness a few minutes, I saw how tightly my arms were clinging onto the blankets, which showed how low the temperature must've dropped to during the night.

"I don't know…" Kevin said, searching the room for a clock but ended up without any luck, "It can't be that early since the sun is already completely over the horizon."

When I looked out the window, I saw the giant ball of flame making its way onto the sky. Contradicting the quietness from last night, the forest surrounding us right now is filled with the chittering of wild animals.

It took us a little less than half an hour to change and get ready for the day. After feeling the chilly air outside, I decided to put on a blue long-sleeve shirt.

Wearing a T-shirt with the same color as his hair, Ben was the first person to burst out of the front door. "The fresh smell of nature is so good!" He said loudly once he's outside.

The rest of us followed him out onto the road shortly as well. Indeed, Ben was right, as we walked to the camp center for breakfast, the leaves from the trees and bushes gave off a pleasant and refreshing scent. "Ah!" The four of us exclaimed, taking deep breaths after deep breaths.

Suddenly, my entire body shook in surprise when I heard someone yelling at us. It was one of the chaperones, "What are you lunatics doing walking so slowly?! Stop daydreaming! You're already late!"

"Oh. Sorry, Mr. Eric." Ben answered, picking up his pace and hurrying over to the white tent, "We overslept a little."

"A *little*?!" Widening his eyes in shock, Mr. Eric repeated the sentence with an extra emphasis on the word "little". "It's already eleven!"

The four of us gasped simultaneously after hearing him, not believing our ears. "Eleven?! Where's the rest of the class then?"

"Where else? Doing activities like always."

Looking at the campus, the only sound I could hear was our talking and the light chirping of insects and birds. I was barely able to see a few people walking around. It was almost as if this entire place was deprived of human voice, "But they're not here." I muttered.

"All of your classmates are in the fieldhouse." Mr. Eric explained, "The ground outside is still wet from the morning dew."

"Ah! I see! Well, we better get going then."

"Just a minute!" He shouted as he held up his hand, signaling for us to come back, "Just want to let you know, we have free lunch today…"

"What does that mean?" Andrew asked from the side.

Mr. Eric towered over him with his overwhelming height and stared down at him with a threatening look, "That's what I was going to tell you before you rudely interrupted me." He hollered. I could see Andrew's body shudder in fear even from where I was standing. Taking a few steps back, he said in a trembling voice, "S-sorry, Mr. Eric."

"As I was saying," Ignoring Andrew's apology, Mr. Eric continued the explanation, "You're free to have lunch in any of the five restaurants on the campus. All you have to do is to show your idea card during checkout and the school will pay for you."

Ben was already off and running to the gymnasium when he yelled, " Sounds cool!" The three of us immediately chased after him once we saw him take off, waving Mr. Eric a goodbye as we left.

The fieldhouse here was a lot bigger than the gym in my school. It had an indoor soccer field, basketball court, hockey rink, and a swimming pool. I saw everyone playing a basketball game when I walked in, and I decided to join them as well. There were a few people sitting on the bleachers to the side of the courts, who I guess either didn't want to play or couldn't play. Ariya, who sat by herself in the first row of the seats, was one of them. I looked at her a few times when I was playing, but her mind was probably drifting to elsewhere and she didn't notice.

I wasn't in there for too long. Once the hour hand of the clock hit twelve o'clock, everyone was dismissed to lunch. "Hey." I said, walking over to Ariya.

"Oh, Kai!" She replied abruptly, looking a little taken back. "I didn't even see you. Did you just get here?"

"About an hour ago."

Looking down at the floor, Ariya muttered, "Oh… I think I wasn't paying attention."

"Don't worry about it." I said as I pushed her wheelchair out of the exit. "So where do you want to eat?"

Once we got outside, however, I realized something was seriously wrong. Instead of seeing the usual blue sky, it was covered with dark clouds, completely obscuring the sun from our view. "What?!" I gasped, "The weather was perfectly fine just an hour ago."

Ariya held her hand up and tried to sense any raindrops. But luckily, there weren't any yet. "Actually, Kai. Can you drop me off at the barbecue restaurant?"

"Am I not coming with you?" I asked.

Shaking her head, Ariya said, "Not this time. I want to do something by myself."

Naturally. I wanted to spend as much time with Ariya as I could, which included eating together. But I knew her well enough to know that if that "something" wasn't important, she wouldn't have told me. "That's alright." I answered without another word.

Luckily, the rain didn't fall yet and we managed to keep ourselves dry on our way to the barbecue restaurant. As we were walking, I noticed Ariya's mood hasn't been too well today. I wanted to chat about something interesting try to loosen her up, but I also didn't want to risk irritating her.

It took us about ten minutes to stroll to the restaurant, which was a sizable wooden hut located next to a pond. After pushing her wheelchair to one of the open tables, I didn't want to bother Ariya any more so I departed.

Now that Ariya was no longer with me, I didn't know what to anymore. I thought maybe Ben or someone else from my room was hanging back in the cabin, but I didn't have any luck finding them once I got there. Walking on the dirt road alone, I suddenly realized something. There were so many fun activities available on the campus, but without Ariya, none of them seemed interesting. That's when I understood how important she was to me. Ariya might not know it, I, myself, didn't even realize it until this moment, but my world without her was as monotonous and grey as the dark sky above.

I stayed inside my cabin, lay on my bed lazily for the rest of the afternoon. I wished someone, I didn't even care who, to push the wooden door open so I wouldn't be lonely anymore, but unfortunately no one did.

Two hours had already passed since I dropped Ariya off at the restaurant. *"What if she's waiting for me because she doesn't have any ways of transportation to get back?"* I jumped out of my bed abruptly, "Who knows what has gotten into her today. I just hope she's not mad at me for being late!"

Stepping out of the wooden hut, I felt a few raindrops hitting my head and skin. It felt cold. No, it felt extremely cold even despite the outside temperature being not even close to freezing. I raced as fast as I could toward the barbecue place, but the rain was beginning to pour down. Eventually, after five minutes of running and almost tripping in the mud multiple times, I was able to see the outline of the wooden building.

Slowing down my footsteps once I got closer, I peeked inside the restaurant through the windows and searched for Ariya. It took a while, but I found her in the corner of the room with someone sitting directly across the table from her. That person was a boy, and he was holding Ariya's hand in his own. His disgusting orange shirt stood out among everyone else's. When I saw his face...

Rumble!

... Both the rainy sky and my trembling heart thundered at the same time.

I snapped around swiftly and darted onto the road, into the pouring rain. Losing myself in both and sadness and anger, everything was a blur after that. I didn't know where I was going, but I didn't care. Anywhere was fine, just not with *them*.

Perhaps she noticed me from inside, Ariya turned her head to the windows just in time and saw me take off with the corner of her vision. She tried to wave at me,"Kai!" yelling out loud, "It's not what it looks like! It's not what you think!"

I shook my head frantically as I sprinted, not paying a single bit of attention to Ariya's voice.

Everything was different before. I used to care about what Ariya had to say. I used to care about Ariya.

But not anymore.

7

I didn't know how long I was running for nor did I remember what I was thinking during that time. In the end, I stopped when I came upon a river and there was nowhere left to go. My body, shirt and hair were utterly drenched. I couldn't tell if it was either from rainfall or from my own sweat.

When I finally had the chance to look around at my surroundings, I realized I was standing next to the stream of water right next to my own cabin. I slowly sat onto the wet meadow and lay my body flat onto the ground, staring straight up at the gloomy sky even with the rain showering right on top of me.

"Why did I have to meet you in the first place, Ariya?" I muttered, "Why do I have to go through all of this?"

I shut my eyelids reluctantly. The beating of the raindrops hitting my face stung like burns after burns, but it didn't bother me. In fact, I wanted it to even more painful so the damage Ariya caused to my heart would feel less throbbing.

Time flew by like a bird darting across the sky. One hour… Soon two hours … passed by in the blink of an eye, so fast that I already lost track. The sky was still equally dark as before, but the rain has weakened to drizzling and almost stopped entirely. From how empty my stomach was right now, I guessed dinner was already over. Nevertheless, I wasn't feeling the least bit of hunger.

Still laying on the grass, I tried to direct my mind to think of something else, but everytime it always circled back to Ariya. "Why?" I groaned.

That's when I heard a noise coming from behind me. It wasn't the chirping of birds nor the chattering of animals. Instead, it was a metallic creaking and someone panting. It sounded really familiar.

I knew who it was without turning around. At first, my original instinct was excitement. But after I thought of what happened earlier, that ecstasy soon vanished into the night sky. I thought she would wait until I said something first, which was what usually happened in conversations between us. This time, however, she was the one who made the first move.

"Kai." She said, her voice was trembling.

If it was before, just hearing her say my name once was enough to make me smile. But my brain was so fuzzy I didn't know whether to feel delighted or angered.

When she knew I wasn't going to give a response, she opened her mouth again, "Everyone's worried about you." She said, finding her voice.

"Liar." I replied without turning around. I didn't want to see anyone not talk to anyone right now, especially not her. With everything that happened since school started, I simply wanted to have some time by myself and clear my mind.

I thought she would turn away after my rejection. After all, she hasn't done anything wrong. So why would she apologize to me and make amends?

"I know how you feel," Ariya continued. I could tell she was absolutely exhaustion through her panting and long pauses in between words. Nonetheless, she spoke in her brightest voice possible and tried to hide her fatigue, "But you mis-"

I chuckled coldly, interrupting her, "No, You don't understand. There's no way you do!" Just thinking about it infuriated me. I started to shout, letting rage take over. "You're the dreamgirl everyone guy on this planet wants! You have the perfect hair, you're tall, you're pretty, you're funny and very open too! But it was a mistake for me to even think that maybe - just maybe an introverted idiot like myself would have a chance with you!"

Ariya made no response to my sudden outburst of emotions.. When I sat up and turned to face her, however, instead of finding the beautiful angel I described earlier, I saw someone with completely drenched clothes and messy hair. She was trying desperately to pull the handles and spin the wheels by herself, but it was barely moving at all.

"What are you doing?" I asked.

She made no reply to my question, instead, Ariya still continued to make her way forward. She was three yards away from where I was standing, but it felt like a distance of ten miles.

I waited for her to say something back, but it never happened. She pursed her lips with a bitter expression and kept her head down the entire time as she pulled herself closer.

"Why?" I groaned painfully, not understanding what she was trying to accomplish by trying to get to me. "Don't you understand? I don't want to see you right now! You've already trod on my feelings enough, just leave me alone." As I got to the end of the sentence, my voice declined so much it resembled more like a pleading than an actual shout.

I didn't realize it earlier, but the rain had already stopped when I looked up at the dark sky. The clouds had cleared away as well, revealing the full moon as it began its climb onto the heavens.

"Because… " Finally after another minute of silence, Ariya opened her mouth just the tiniest crack and whispered into my ears slowly and softly, with tears welling up in her eyes, "I love you."

Out of all of the words in the world, those three were the ones I was expecting to hear the least. "Cut the crap!" I exploded in anger, too shocked to process anything in my head, "Now you're making fun of me?! You and Ben were just…on a date! Now you say you love me? How do you expect me to believe that?"

"It's like you said before!" Finally reaching her limits, Ariya started to yell as well, "You're an introverted, unsocial idiot! You don't have good grades! You're not tall, not athletic either! But if love isn't the reason, then why in the world would I choose you over everyone else to help me around in school!? Why would I waste two hours of my life this afternoon trying to find and reach you!? It's because I want to be with you! I want to hear you speak! I want to hear words come out of your mouth! I love you from the bottom of my heart!"

To those questions and statement, I had no response. I didn't know why I wasn't completely overwhelmed with joy yet. After all, the girl I had a crush on just told me she loved me as well.

"Last Thursday, when we were hanging out in the arcade, I love how you tried dancing with me even though it was your first time." Ariya said, slowing down her voice.

With the sudden change in her voice, I was taken off guard and didn't know how to reply. "No…" I squeezed the single word out of my mouth.

"On that same day, even though we had just met, I love how you cared about me so much and how you knew I wanted to have one of the sweet potatoes. When I bit into it, it was the sweetest thing I've ever tasted in my life."

"N-no…" I shook my head in a frenzy, "I wasn't…"

"I love how you were thoughtful enough to bring me a piece of cake when you visited me in the hospital for the first time. I had almost forgotten what happiness tasted like, until you came."

I didn't want to listen to Ariya anymore. I wanted to lose my both of my ears so I could no longer hear her voice, the voice which once warmed my soul. Right then, under the shimmering moonlight, Ariya was pouring every single drop of her feeling to me, but unfortunately none of them were reaching me.

"Stop." I muttered again.

"I love how your fingers caressed my hair. No one has ever done my own hair for me before, especially someone like you."

I didn't even know what to say at this point. Glancing at the forest and looking for words to answer Ariya with, a little bird flying in midair caught my attention. It circled us for a few seconds, then landed onto the grass swiftly. "T-that's only because I had to help Mia…" My eyes followed the bird as it hopped around the grassfield.

Ariya shook her head reluctantly, "I also love how your face was blushing when you asked me out for dinner that night in my hospital room. I tried to hide my nervousness and looked composed on the outside, but my heart was already thumping out of my chest. "It was the first time someone asked me to go out with him. I bet I was even more anxious than you were."

Staring into the moon's reflection in the river behind me, wholehearted emotions gushed out of her mouth. On the contrary to myself, her voice reminded me of ringing chimes. Quiet but powerful, they were making their way into my bruised heart one word at a time.

"I might not have said so, but during the lockdown when you ran up to the room I was in and knocked on the doors, I was never more excited to see someone in my life. Back then, when I saw you knocking on the door, you were my hope, you were the reason that I'm still alive today... You were my life."

"..."

"With everything that we went through, I now know what loving someone truly meant." Taking a slight pause, Ariya turned her head to face me and looked directly into my eyes, "Love isn't just simply asking someone out for lunch or dinner. Love isn't spending a single afternoon with them and walking around the city holding hands. It's more than that... it's when you are willing to give up your own life if it means the other could survive. it's when you are willing to live for the sake of someone else."

I didn't even know tears were flowing out of my eyes until Ariya's hand flew up and wiped them from my face. "That's...nice. I agree." I muttered, my hard feelings toward her from earlier all disappeared.

Pausing a little, she said, "And the person who taught me that, was you."

"Ariya, I—"

Cutting me off, she reached out with her arms and looped them around my head, pulling my face directly to hers. It all happened too quick. Before I had the chance to realize what was going on, my lips were already intertwined with hers.

Despite both of us being soaking wet, the sensation I felt on my mouth resembled warmth and filled with life. After a few seconds, Ariya gradually pulled her face away from mine, both of us staring into the other's eyes. She just told me everything single drop of her feelings, and I wanted to confess to her my feelings as well. But in the end, I figured it wasn't necessary. Because this kiss, this mutual sensation on our lips, along with all the time we've spent with each other, already conveyed all of our genuine emotions.

Shattering the silence between us once again, Ariya said, "I've loved you since the first day of school last week."

I nodded quietly with Ariya's arms in mine. "Me too." I said at last.

"No…" she suddenly spoke up again, sounding a little different this time, "it was since that time when I met you four years ago, under the meteor shower." As Ariya finished that last sentence, her voice was as soft and charming as a prayer.

— —

Four years ago (Ariya's past)

"Kai…Kai! " I yelled the name of the boy lying on the ground right in front of me, the name of the boy who just sacrificed himself and pushed me out of danger. "Don't go… I didn't even get to say thank you."

There was nothing I could do besides to stare at his body as the puddle or dark crimson grew larger and larger besides him. I placed my hand onto his chest, and let out a sigh of relief when I felt the slight beating of his heart. It wasn't strong, but he was alive.

"Please… not you too! My parents were already enough! I don't want to lose someone else!" I said silently, as I knelt on the ground next to him. When my hand brushed against his short black hair, I was surprised to find it a lot softer than I expected.

After almost an hour of silently beside him, sirens and ambulances were finally pulling up onto the street. I hurried outside, carrying the unconscious boy in my arms. He was taller than me only by a little bit, and looked fairly skinny. But he nevertheless weighed more than I expected. It was tiring and took me a while, but I managed to make it out of the half-destroyed building without tripping over.

"Please sir!" I shouted desperately as I rushed over to one of the people driving an ambulance, "Take him to the hospital! He's my friend! But I don't know if…"

The man looked down at me from the driver's seat, "Don't worry," he said, gesturing me to get on the vehicle, "your friend is going to be alright."

"Oh… Thank goodness!" Letting out a huge gulp of air, I asked, "Can I come too?"

"Of course, you're gonna want to keep him company, right?"

Once we arrived in front of the enormous white building in about half an hour, Kai was immediately taken to the emergency room, and I was sent to a regular room for my small injuries and bruises. While there wasn't anything interesting and fun to do during my stay at the hospital, it wasn't a pain either. I was happy that they provided me with shelter and three meals a day. Unfortunately, even though I was constantly asking, I didn't even get to see Kai once. The doctors told me he was in critical condition and couldn't see anyone. There was a chance that he would never be able to walk again if the treatment failed.

That night, before sleeping, I knelt on my bed and whispered to the heavens with full sincerity, "Please let me see Kai again! Please let me have the chance to run around and play with him!"

I rushed downstairs the next morning to the doctor's office and asked about how Kai's surgery went. To my pleasant surprise, I received good news on his success. The doctor said it would take him a few months to completely heal, and then he asked me to help Kai out and to push him around because he needed to constantly be in a wheelchair, which I immediately agreed to.

I entered Kai's room an hour after my talk with the medic. Surrounded four sides of white walls with no windows, the only furnitures in there were a table, a chair, and a bed. It was the plainest of the plain. The dark haired boy was sitting in his black wheelchair, already waiting for me. Dressed in a simple white shirt and some blue pants, almost the entire lower half of his body was covered in bandages, tightly wrapping his waist and legs.

"Hey." He said in a feeble voice. It was unusually quiet despite his smile and trying to sound as cheerful as possible. "You're still here?."

Walking over to where Kai was sitting and plopping myself into a chair, "I know how loneliness feels like. Staying with you is the least I could do to help my savior."

I could tell he got a little choked up after hearing my response. He wiped his eyes with the sleeves of his shirt and tried to avert his gaze away from mine, "T-thanks… it feels a lot better to have a friend with me."

"It's the same with me too." I said, "at least we have each other to talk to…"

Silence permeated throughout the room and neither of us opened our mouths for quite a long time after that. Staring at the floor, I would occasionally glance up at the boy sitting in front of me. His eyes were closed, but his mind drifted off to somewhere else. I didn't want to interrupt his thoughts, so I kept quiet as well.

"So…" Kai started to say, breaking the stillness, "What are you going to do now?"

"Aren't we going to stay together?" I asked.

"Well, I guess the first thing I have to look for my family. I still don't know if they survived."

"Oh." I muttered, a little surprised and sad to hear him say this. Just when I thought I've found someone who I thought would stay with me, not forever, but at least for quite a long time, that person was going to push me away. Upon meeting him, I imagined the two of us would accompany each other as we traveled the world. But what could I do about it? It was his decision and his life. "T-that's good of you to still care about your family so much." I managed to say.

"Hey, don't get the wrong idea," Seeing my downed expression, Kai spoke up softly, "I'm not going to leave you. You're coming with me, that is, if you want to."

He might not have realized it, but those words were the words I wanted to hear the most. Ever since my parents passed away in the Meteors, I had almost given up on this cold-blooded world. But it was always Kai who showed me there was still faith, and it was Kai who showed me there were still reasons to living. And for me, one of the reasons was getting to be with him. "Of course…" I muttered.

"I still need you to push me around, remember? If you just left me by myself, I wouldn't be able to survive. So I physically can't live without you."

From Kai's words, he made it sound like I was sacrificing a lot on being with him. But that wasn't true at all. In reality, I would've asked and begged Kai to let me stay with him. "No worries." I affirmed him, "I'll go wherever you go, do whatever you do, and live whatever life you live."

He nodded, his eyes were already welling up with tears, "This cruel world already took the lives of the lives of the two people most important to you, and almost your own life as well. But from this day forth. Let's show this world that we're going to live on. Meteors, earthquakes, fires, bring them on, nature! Because no matter what disasters you bring our way, we will survive."

It might've been a little nonsensical to hear a kid who was still in fifth-grade say this, but I was really impressed back then. Right after seeing all the destruction the Meteors had caused to the city, Kai was already courageous enough to declare this. As I stared at him in awe, I thought to myself, "Wow. There is really nothing Kai can't do. I wish I would be able to say that someday."

However, my renewed sense of freedom and hope soon vanished into thin air, as they told us the next day that Kai and I were being transported to another facility. And this place was going to be our home for the entirety of next year.

Kai and I were woken up exceptionally early the next day and were told to hurry up into a private bus as the sun just peeked it's way over the horizon. We knew we were going to another hospital, but that was all. With the tight schedule we were on, they told us to not bring anything since every necessity will be provided over there.

At first, I thought it was going to be a short ride as we were probably being transported to somewhere nearby. But as hours and hours passed by and the view of city was already in the rear window, I found myself getting more and more nervous.

Kai, who sat next to me in his usual wheelchair, spoke up when he noticed my trembling body, "It's gonna be alright. It's only another hospital."

"If it's just a regular hospital, then why are we going so far away? There are plenty of hospitals in the city."

"Maybe... for better equipments?" He guessed.

"How would some place in the middle of a forest ave better equipments than a modern city?"

Kai sighed, "Look, I understand. You're scared, and I am too. To tell you the truth, I don't know anything about the place either. Just try to take our mind off it and think about something else. We're going to find out everything once we arrive." I glanced out the window and said, "you can look at the passing trees and animals outside."

I nodded and listened to his suggestion. With neither of us talking, the back of the vehicle was silent besides the mumbled conversation coming from the front. Finally, after another hour of bus ride, we arrived at in front of a huge white structure surrounded by tall fences. We weren't allowed to ask any questions, but this resembled nothing like an ordinary hospital from the outside look.

After the bus pulled into what appeared to be a garage, Kai and I were told to get off and were escorted inside the building.

The first thing I realized upon entering the "hospital" was that we weren't the only ones there. Many other kids, mostly a few years older than us, were apparently having lessons in a classroom. A few minutes later, the two of us were taken to our dorm rooms, which were located on the fifth of seven floors and they were connected on the inside despite our gender differences.

The rooms were similar to other dormitories. It had a bed, a bathroom, a chair, and a table. There was something lying on the desk when I walked in, after reading it over, I realized it was my schedule of the week.

I had regular classes in the morning, lunch at noon, and some research activity I had to participate in during the afternoon. It wasn't even that different from a regular boarding school's schedule. Even though I still wasn't sure why we were here, I was a little relieved to find out Kai had the same exact classes as me, which meant we would be together for at least most of the time.

Because it was our first day here, we didn't have anything planned for the rest of the afternoon. Surprisingly, we have quite a lot of freedom. We were free to wander around the place with no adult supervision. I would push Kai with me wherever I went and the two of us sat by ourselves during meals. Every once in a while someone would point and is and murmur a few words, but Kai told me to not pay any attention and keep on eating my sandwich.

We spent the rest of the evening in our dorm with the room connecting the two rooms open. I was glancing through some of the books in my room and Kai was getting familiar with the map of the entire area. However, when it was nine o'clock and I already helped Kai into his bed, I was tossing and turning, unable to fall asleep.

For that first night, along with many other nights, Kai would comfort me every time whenever I couldn't sleep. I would sometimes go to his room and we'd sit next to each other, quietly talking to each other about our lives before this incident happened. "Why were we so unlucky enough to have this disaster happen to us?" Kai had exclaimed once, "Why did this have to happen? Why is the reality so cruel?!"

I didn't have an exact answer for his question at that exact moment, but I felt like I was on my way to discovering the answer.

For the next three-hundred days after our arrival, both Kai and I underwent a change for a new and stricter lifestyle. We would get up everyday at seven, have classes until twelve, lunch until one, researches until six, dinner until seven, and lights out at nine. We were like machines, trained to perform these tasks without any exceptions. There wasn't even any bonuses for if we behaved well and didn't cause any trouble. However, there were punishments. Any sort of misconduct will result in the loss of a meal or could even get us in solitary confinement, which could last for a whole week.

The first few weeks were the hardest to live through. The tortuous studies the staff conducted on our skin and body were nasty and disturbing at the lightest. They would ambush us with needles and retract our own blood for research. It was later revealed that the reason we were transported here was because we were two of the very few people who were directly exposed to the Meteors. Along with the homesickness I felt when I thought about the tragedy of my parents, tears would end up in my eyes every morning.

But despite everything, the person who always calmed me down was Kai. He'd hug me tight with his arms, letting the warmth of his body sink into me, and we would stay there until my teardrops felt like it was going to harden into the skin.

At first, I didn't even think about what Kai was feeling and what was going on in his head, but it all changed when I suddenly woke up in the middle of the night once and heard the sound of Kai's sobbing coming from the other room.

I didn't know what I was waiting for, but I sat quietly on my bed in the dark. Maybe it was because I didn't know what to do; maybe it was because I haven't ever seen Kai like this before, or maybe it was simply because I wanted him to release some of his stored-up feelings out so everything would be easier for him. It could've been any of those reasons, but I wasn't sure what to do next.

Do I go to his room and talk to him? Or do I ignore Kai and go back to sleep? Of course, I knew which one was the right choice to make. But before I was able to produce any sound with my wide-opened mouth, a question popped into my head: Is my voice warm and soothing enough to relieve some of the pressure he's having?

I clearly knew that there was no way I would know the answer, but what if he didn't want to hear me? Or even worse, what if I was the source of his anguish?

With all of these uncertainties, reluctantly shut my mouth and laid back onto my bed. Despite so many attempts of mine to fall asleep after that, I couldn't do so. Perhaps it was self-consciousness at work. In the end, I finally worked up enough courage, "Kai?"

No response

"Kai? What's wrong? Why are you crying?" I asked again as I walked over to him. His face was looking at the other side of the room.

"A-Ariya…" He spoke up after a delay, "I sometimes get scared too."

I didn't know how to respond, so I just stayed quiet.

"Yeah, of course." He continued, wiping the tears in his eyes, "Don't think of me like an adult or anything, I'm the same age as you. Honestly, I try my best to look composed when I'm around you. But on the inside, I'm just as frightened as you are."

Ever since I met him, I've always thought of Kai as someone who knew everything and wasn't afraid of everything. So to hear him say he was pretending was definitely a huge surprise, "Why were you faking it then?"

"Because, " he hesitated for a second, "it's like I said earlier. You might've thought of me as a burden."

"What?" I exclaimed loudly, "I would never think of you that way!"

"I know, I know. That was my bad." Kai said, waving his hand to calm me down.

The fact that Kai was still worrying about me ditching him out a little unease into my mind. But I was glad he told me and clarified everything in the end. "Don't worry about it. But make sure to tell me everything you feel, just like me talking to you about my emotions." I said, as I turned around to leave, "it'll make me happy too."

"Hey." He nodded and said suddenly, "can you stay with me tonight?"

That was the first time ever where Kai asked me to accompany him for the night. Even though it was the smallest of questions, I didn't know why, but I felt my heart shook. "Of course." I answered quickly.

Neither of said a single word to each other after that. When I climbed onto his bed, I turned around to face the windows on the opposite side of the room, the moon shone brightly on my face, but I didn't mind the light at all. With Kai's slight breathing in the background, I slowly shut my eyes as well.

"The Meteors impacted the Earth so we could meet. It was our destiny. If it didn't happen in the first place, I wouldn't even have met you. And that single reason is enough to make me thankful that this was the reality."

Some days were eventful, while some were not. After a couple of months, Kai's injury was able to recover and the period of time after that was the highlight of our painful year. Without his wheelchair, we ran inside the building in our free time, which was one hour after dinner, and played all sorts of games together. Even though we had to endure so many hardships, there was always something I looked forward to everyday.

Just when it looked like we were finally getting used to our life here, everything all came to a sudden end when the calendar stroke the ten month mark.

One morning, we were woken up at the crack of dawn and were hustled into the research room. Despite the outside still mostly dark, the inside of the building was completely lit up. People were running all over the place, both kids and adults. From the shouting of the staff members, I heard that the government has found out about this place and they were shutting this facility down. I tried asking them why, and why were we going to the research at a time like this, but they paid no attention and ignored me.

Once we arrived at the lab, they took Kai to a different room. "No!" I yelled, stretching my arm out as far as I could in an attempt to reach him, but it was in vain. I heard him say something back at me, but his voice died out with all of the commotions surrounding us.

The staff told me to lie on the table, similar to the countless times I've done before. Only this was different. After the equipment hovered over my head and turned itself on, my vision of my surroundings suddenly became hazy, then they all turned into a screen of white. My consciousness evaporated into the thin air, and so did all my memories. Memories of this facility, memories of the year I've spent here, memories of the classes, memories of the experiments, memories of the time Kai and I spent together, and eventually, memories of my best friend himself, all turned into nothingness.

Back then, I thought that was the last time I would ever see him again. But little did I know that we would somehow miraculously reunite, four years later…

"Ariya," I whispered quietly into the girl's ears as she sat in her black wheelchair. With the occasional chirping of animals and the forest enveloping us, I knelt on the ground and the two of us were still in the position of our hug from earlier. "It's just a dream." I said to her.

I stared directly into her amethyst eyes as she slowly lifted them open. "Kai… I…" Tears started selling up as soon as she choked on her words.

I interrupted Ariya, bringing her even closer to m,, "I understand you, I saw, I was there."

She clutched her arms around me and dug her face into my chest, "Kai!"

"Yeah?" I answered as I softly caressed her golden hair.

"T-thank you!"

"For?"

"Thank you for buying me that sweet potato… Thank you for bringing me those pieces of cake… Thank you for taking me out for dinner that night… Thank you for saving me in that shooting… Thank you for saving me four years ago." After a slight hesitation, "No, thank you… for everything!"

8

I thought of everything that happened between Ariya and me that night before I went to bed, and I was pondering whether I should tell Ben about all of this. However, he was nowhere to be seen even when the lights wer0e shut out. I asked my two cabinmates, but they both said the last time Ben was seen was before dinner and they weren't sure where he went.

"He probably had a soccer game scheduled and he had to leave the trip early." Andrew muttered as he lay on his bed, tossing a water bottle in the air and trying to catch it, fumbling.

I nodded, "Yeah, you're probably right." Turning my head around, closed my eyes and went to sleep, not even sure if I was delighted or dejected to hear about his absence.

When I woke up the next morning, the previous night still felt really hazy. "Was it a dream?" I muttered to myself as I spun out of my bed and got onto my feet. The first thing I saw was Ben's empty bed next to mine, and all that did was assured me that this was the reality after all. As I tried to breathe in a gulp of the fresh morning air, I realized I couldn't. "Man... I must've caught a cold after staying in the rain for so long. My nose is stuffed and my entire body is aching"

After glancing at Andrew and Kevin, who were still snoring in their beds, I got dressed hastily, went to the restroom, and headed for the main tent by myself for breakfast, just in time to be one of the first people there.

As soon as they saw me from their table, the teachers were already waving at me asking how my night was. I didn't want to get into a conversation so early in the morning, so I responded with a "It was fine." and walked toward the other direction.

Not much happened in the morning, as everyone was getting ready for the hike up a nearby mountain, which is going to take place early in the afternoon. I had just finished packing my backpack, filled with snacks, water bottles, and other small gadgets, when the rhythmic chime of the bell rang twelve times. And my cabinmates ran toward the main tent for a meetup as soon as we heard it. By then, most of my soreness had already vanished, and I couldn't help but smile when my sight landed on Ariya for the first time of the day.

At first, I was sure what to say when I approached her, considering our confessions that took place the night before. In the end, I just settled on a "How was your night?" and carried on the conversation like normal.

"Pretty good." Ariya answered, shuddering, "Besides that fact that my roommates spent an entire half-hour lecturing me on why I shouldn't have exhausted myself last night in the rain when I was trying to get to you."

"At least they care about you." I smiled, "Anyways, are you ready for the hiking trip? I bet it'll be a lot of fun!"

Instead of high-fiving me like I expected her to, however, Ariya sank like a deflated balloon. "I don't think I can go." She muttered, her face staring at the brown leaves piling up on the ground.

"Wait why?"

"Well… look at my wheelchair. The teachers said it would be a huge waste of energy to push me, even on the paved walkway for vehicles. And plus, they said it would be easy for me to get hurt." Ariya explained.

"Ah come on!" I exclaimed, clenching my fist, "Even if you have someone who's willing to push you up the mountain? It would be so beautiful up there! We can see the sunset together!"

Ariya tried faking a smile to comfort me, she said, "Don't worry about it, we'll share plenty of sunsets together, after we get home from the trip and my injury recovers. But to answer your question, I did ask them the same thing , and they said yes. Unfortunately though, before you arrived, I already asked most of the class if they were willing to lend me a hand. Although some of them wanted to, they had other friends and business they had to take care of."

"Aha!" I shouted and smiled, this time a genuine one. "The key word is *before I came here!*"

"Really?!" Ariya whispered."

"Gladly!" I replied, "It took you two hours to reach me last night, didn't it? And you managed to do it. So it'll only be a piece of cake for me!"

"T-thanks…" She whispered lightly, with a pair of watery eyes.

Suddenly, a teacher's booming voice through the megaphone brought the two of us back to reality, "Alright kids! Follow me, we're going to begin our hike!"

Gently laying my hands on Ariya's wheelchair handles and pushing it in the direction of the mountain, I was a little surprised on how much it actually weighed, *"Don't worry, I can do this…"* I muttered to myself, *"For Ariya."*

Luckily for us, the hike started off nice and easy. We actually didn't take the hardcore route, which included many wall climbs and other difficult sections, because they were afraid not everyone is capable of completing the strenuous tasks. Instead, the teachers instructed us to stay on the main route, which was a paved road that lead all the way up to the top.

Besides a few occasional bumps which made steering Ariya's wheelchair difficult, the way up the mountain was surprisingly beautiful. We were right next to some huge waterfalls, close enough to actually touch them with our fingers. Ariya even playfully splashed me with the freezing spring water, getting my clothes wet; but all I did was laugh and made a mental note to get even with her later on in the trip.

One time, when we had just reached the second waterfall, Ariya spotted numerous number of rainbows on top of each other and immediately grabbed my hand, which was lying on her wheelchair handles, and exclaimed, "Kai! Look at that! It's so beautiful!"

Following the direction of her pointing arm, all I could do was let out a quiet gasp as I saw the spectacle she was talking about. Indeed, like Ariya said, it was really gorgeous. Not only did the colors of each rainbow cleanly match the previous, each individual rainbows also meticulously overlapped with the next one. My classmates didn't want such a wondrous sight to slip away, as they all got out their cell phones and cameras out to capture this moment before we continued on our way up the mountain.

The class made one more stop along our journey by a nice little town situated around the middle of the mountainside. If I were to describe the scenery I witnessed that morning with a single word, it would be "tranquil". The cool breezes blowing past, the wooden houses, shacks, yards, and most importantly, the unbroken tranquility everything was surrounded in. Some of the villagers made their way over to the shrine gate to welcome us, but everyone talked in their lowest voicest minimum voice, even my noisy classmates, as if they were afraid to shatter the quietness of the afternoon.From where I was standing, I could see the very top of the mountain peaking over the clouds. With the trees blocking off parts of the sunshine, I turned my head around and stared into the distance. Out there, into the distance, past the miles and miles of green forests and thick trees, almost past the horizon and beyond my sight, lay the very tip of the beautiful city. It made me wonder, *"Nature sure is pretty, isn't it?"*

We wandered aimlessly around for a short period of time, free to do whatever we want within the village. Because this mountain attracts a considerable number of tourists each year, there were shops located throughout the place for people to purchase souvenirs. There was a wood carving of a bear climbing a tree in one of the stores which caught my eyes, but the costly price tag made me drop the whole thing. During this entire time, Ariya sat on the wheelchair in front of me, not saying a word. Perhaps she noticed the beads of sweat dripping from my face, or my shaking arms and hands, she didn't make another request to go anywhere else and check out any more things, to which I was thankful for.

When the class finally departed from the town, it was already almost three in the afternoon, and I thought we were almost at the top already. However, when I looked up the side of the mountain, I was shocked to see that we still have a long way to go. With the path zigzagging in and out of the forest, and getting increasingly smaller the higher we get, I was having second thoughts on whether I was able to make it all the way up there without fainting from exhaustion. I didn't know what I was doing this for, nor why I was stressing so much just to reach the peak. But whenever I looked at the girl sitting in the wheelchair before me, all my laziness and tiredness vanished without a trace. I managed to continue for another hour or so, until there was only about one fifth of the way left. When I saw a bench under some shade, I couldn't help but to make a beeline for it, explaining to Ariya, "Give me a minute, I need a little break." After an entire afternoon of walking and standing, I finally relieved my legs of their duty, even if it's only for a short while. Looking up at the orange leaves falling from the branches dangling midair, I saw Ariya looking at me, giggling playfully. I couldn't help but to give an awkward smile back her way.

After letting the teachers know that the class didn't have to wait for us, Ariya made her way over to me by spinning the wheels herself and handed me a bottle of water. "Here, drink this. You gotta stay hydrated."

Without another word, I gulped the entire bottle down with record time. Letting out a refreshing gasp and thanked her when I finished. "Alright! Let's get going!" I said, getting back to my feet.

The two of us resumed our climb up the mountain; but we didn't try to catch up to the group. First because I was still too exhausted to run while pushing a wheelchair; Second, it was also because I felt like spending more time with Ariya away from the noisy group seemed like a more romantic choice.

Soon after we got back onto the road, the sun began its descent down the clear blue sky; and we decided to pick up the pace. The higher and higher we got, I noticed the thinner the leaves and the vegetation became; and the more chilly the temperature dropped to. Without stopping once for the remainder of the climb, we finally reached the peak after a strenuous last stretch, just in time to catch sight of the sunset.

The top of the mountain was shaped like a circle, about the size of two of a classroom combined. It wasn't a whole lot of space, but by no means was it crowded either. By the time we arrived, however, our classmates had already left and were nowhere to be seen.

There were fences surrounding the circular enclosure at the top. But when I walked over to the edge, I could tell that I was standing on a cliff with a steep drop right in front of me."Phew!" I exclaimed, and backed off from the side, letting my mind blank out as I tried to relax myself, and felt the gradual breeze brushing against my cheeks. I walked toward the stone bench in the middle of the enclosure, parked the wheelchair next to me, and finally relieved my legs of their duty. "Well, this is a nice view." I muttered, staring into the distance.

Even though it was barely evening, the stars were already making its way onto the clear, tangerine-colored sky. With the moon rising in the east and sun setting in the west, the quiet scenery in front of us really reminded me of a picturesque scene from a movie. "So Ariya," I said, it was like all of my fatigue had disappeared, "What are you going to do once we get back? Where are you going to live?"

I could tell she got a little startled at my sudden question, it was clear that she hadn't figured that far into the future yet. "I-I don't know…" She muttered.

"Good, so you don't have any plans, "laying my hand on her shoulder, I answered cheerfully, "Wanna come live with me and Mia? My parents are always working in other cities or overseas, so it's only me and my little sister taking care of the entire place. It gets a little lonely sometimes."

I could tell that her eyes lit up after hearing my invitation, but she calmed herself down and asked, "Are you sure if it won't be a bother?"

"Of course not!" I smiled, "For the one trillionth time, you're never a bother. We can walk to school together everyday; and come back together too."

"That would be really nice." Ariya replied, "Thank you."

Neither of us said another word to each other after that. We simply sat there, me on the bench and Ariya in her chair to my right. There were a myriad of sounds surrounding us: the chirping of birds and insects, the rustling of leaves, and the tinkling of the rushing spring river. I guess what they said were true, time flies when you're having fun. Because just after what I felt like was only a minute, the sun had completely vanished down the horizon and night loomed in over us.

"Oh shoot! Look at the time!" I shouted after finally taking a look at my watch. "We better hurry up and get down the mountain before the class gets worried."

Ariya nodded hesitantly in response. I quickly stood up and made our way to the exit of the peak. Even though there were a few streetlamps scattered across the route down, the visibility was still minimal. One single peek on the dark road ahead was all it took to send chills down my spine. I didn't know if going down the mountain at a time like this would be the best choice, but I didn't want us two to get stranded on the mountain without food for the whole night. "Here we go."

The first part of our descent was relatively smooth sailing. There were a couple of sections where the roads were steeper than normal, but they weren't anything impossible to accomplish. Sometimes I would feel like we were being watched by animals; sometimes I'd hear the howling of a wolf; and other times I'd hear a rusting in the dark. I tried not to think closely to what the noises were, because I knew they were only going to make me paranoid.

After a few stumbles and bruises, we found our way back to the waterfall located about halfway down the mountain, where we stopped earlier and caught sight of the overlaying rainbows. With the dim light the streetlamps was able to provide, I could tell It was still the same waterfall, but it felt different when it's dark out. The mud on the ground was damp from the spilling water and last night's rain, and we were walking by the section right next to the cataract without any railing; that was when I slipped on some moss and fell onto the ground; my heart immediately sank. Because of my sudden movements, I lost control of Ariya's wheelchair and it rolled off the open cliff and straight down the enormous drop. Fortunately, Ariya was able to jump down in the last second, and reached over to a nearby rock sticking out of the terrain. That wasn't the end, however. Her body was now dangling in the air, with the nearest solid ground being a hundred feet under her. "Kai!" Ariya shouted in pain. "Save me!"

It took me a little bit to process what had just happened. But Ariya's sharp voice brought me back to reality. "Hold on!" I answered, making my way over to the edge of the cliff without falling down too. I first placed one of my hands onto a nearby branch of a tree, reaching down with the other, I exclaimed, "Grab it with your other hand!" I wasn't sure if her other injured hand was strong enough to do the task, but it was the only option.

From the terrified expression on her face, I could tell that it wasn't easy. But she tried her hardest and did what I told her to. I felt her warmth the moment her hand touched mine; she was clutching onto me with all her remaining strength, refusing to let go. *Dear God… Please lend me strength… To save her one last time. I promise I will be content with everything I have … I just need her to be alive… Please.*

Putting in every ounce of strength I have, I gave Ariya one last yank. Instead of saving her, however, that was when the branch I was holding on to finally gave way. Everything after that happened so fast, I didn't have time to process it through. I wasn't sure If I genuinely didn't remember, or my mind trying to forget it; but all I recall was me grabbing onto a rock on the edge for dear life; as I watched her body plummet into the watery abyss. "Ariya!!!" I howled and wailed until I was able to taste my own blood in my throat. The echo of my cries resounded throughout the entire mountain.

It has been two days since my class returned from the mountain trip, and those two days spent in my bedroom by myself, with the shades drawn. I would always wake up and have food on my desk, which I assumed was Mia helping me out. And I appreciated her not bothering me once after I arrived.

I spent all of the time lying in bed, and not a single minute went by without me thinking of her. How Ariya's charming voice was like the red on the color pallete of my life; her sorrow was the blue; her humorous jokes would be nature's green, her tears were the maroon red. "I wasn't able to save her. I didn't even say 'I love you' back." I whispered as I stood up, and finally walked out of my room for the first time.

It looked like it was early morning from the half-dimmed, half-bright light coming through the windows, and I could hear a few birds chirping and flying around. Sitting myself down on the couch in the living room, I saw yesterday's town newspaper with the headline: " High School Orientation Trip Turned into Disaster!" The last picture taken of Ariya before she went missing was included right under. At first, it really pained me to even take a peek, but then I realized I've missed something important once I saw here more clearly, "Your smile," I said, "That smile of yours, was like the shining gold of my color palette."

Outside, the red-feathered bird leapt off the windowsill and took flight into the distance, under dawn's first rays of light.

~ The End ~